IT TOOK AN EARTHQUAKE

IT TOOK AN EARTHQUAKE

A Novel

Miriam J. Walker

iUniverse, Inc.
New York Lincoln Shanghai

It Took An Earthquake

Copyright © 2006 by Miriam J. Walker

iUniverse books may be ordered through booksellers or by contacting:

iUniverse
2021 Pine Lake Road, Suite 100
Lincoln, NE 68512
www.iuniverse.com
1-800-Authors (1-800-288-4677)

ISBN-13: 978-0-595-40122-2 (pbk)
ISBN-13: 978-0-595-84503-3 (ebk)
ISBN-10: 0-595-40122-8 (pbk)
ISBN-10: 0-595-84503-7 (ebk)

Printed in the United States of America

I dedicate "It Took An Earthquake" to the Town of Marblehead, Massachusetts, where I was born some two hundred years after the birth of Agnes Surriage. Like Agnes, I was taken from Marblehead as a teen-ager, but I remember it well from Fort Sewall to the Lead Mills—its marvelous beaches, its churches, its schools, its cemeteries where several generations of my people are buried, its people, and the awesome contributions of its citizens to the growth and preservation of the United States from before the American Revolution. It has been a labor of love for me to retell Marblehead's most romantic love story for the edification and entertainment of new generations of readers.

—Miriam J. Walker
nee Miriam J. Dennis

P R O L O G U E

―――――――――― ▼ ――――――――――

In 1767 Sir Charles Henry (Harry) Frankland had once again made the voyage from the Massachusetts Bay Colony in North America to Bath, England. He had hoped the soothing waters of the Roman baths which gave the city its name would restore his health, but they did not, and now he was too weak to get to them. He was, in fact, confined to his bed. His still-beautiful, still-adoring wife Agnes, Lady Frankland, sat by his side.

Harry's mind and memory were as keen as ever, and he spent his days reminiscing about the high points of his life and illustrious career. Agnes sat silent when he talked of matters that were his alone. She contributed her own recollections of those events they had shared, and they were many, including the terrible earthquake that impacted so powerfully on the couple's life back in 1755. She noticed that Harry's eyes grew just a bit brighter and his voice a bit stronger whenever he harked back to the days just prior to his leaving Bengal, India, to sail to England to be educated. It is there that we begin this biography of the man who was a great grandson of Oliver Cromwell, the first-born son of the Governor of the East India Company in Bengal, the nephew of The Lord High Admiral of the British Fleet, and himself the 4th Baronet of Thirsk in the North Riding of York.

CHAPTER 1

▼

In two more days, twelve-year-old Harry Frankland, son of the Governor of the British East India Company in Bengal, would be leaving India, his family, and all he had ever known. He lay on his bed and thought about the voyage to England that he would soon embark upon. While he was eager to see the great ship on which he would sail, he was equally reluctant to say farewell to his family. He looked forward to meeting his Uncle Thomas and moving into Great Thirkleby Hall, the Frankland ancestral home in the North Riding of York, where he would be educated in the manner befitting a young man of his aristocratic background, but he couldn't help wondering what he would be studying, what his tutors would be like, and how he would be treated in his uncle's home. He vaguely remembered seeing his uncle years earlier, but he had not met his uncle's second wife or his cousins. He knew the climate, the landscape, the architecture, and the culture of England would be quite different from what he was used to in Bengal, but he could have no idea of what lay ahead for him: his future career as Collector of the Port of Boston in The Massachusetts Bay Colony in 1742, or his subsequent romance with a beautiful girl who scrubbed floors at the Fountain Inn in Marblehead, or the effect on his life of a devastating earthquake which would take place in Lisbon, Portugal in 1755.

How would he spend these last days? He tried reading, but his own books had already been packed, and those of his brothers were not to his liking. A nap would help to pass these hours, but he could not get to sleep.

He sought out Arun, the Indian servant he called "Uncle", to see if there was something he could do to help him, but Arun assured him everything was under control. For lack of anything better to do, Harry took his younger brother Robert's toy sailboat to the fountain behind the Franklands' home and pretended it was the one on which he would be sailing. He visualized the roundhouse where his cabin would be located, the Captain's quarters, and the steerage section. He hoped Captain Van Vleet was as considerate a man as his father had indicated, especially when it came to crossing the Equator. He hoped this ship's crew was not as rough as some his father told him about. He hoped he would not have to face seasickness or storms at sea or pirates. Most of all he imagined the ship's sails filled with wind as the vessel made its way out to the Bay of Bengal and into the Atlantic Ocean.

He went for a long walk, stopping to talk with many of his school friends who were playing outside. When these boys learned what lay ahead for Harry, they had many questions to ask, which he was only too glad to answer to the best of his ability. When the boys were envious, Harry felt elevated, special, as though he was the only boy ever to be singled out for such honors. When they showed relief that it was not they who were leaving their families and friends, he was quickly brought back to the reality of his situation. He finally turned homeward, not entirely sure if the walk had helped his mood. It had, at least, filled the time until dinner was due to be served.

Arriving at his home, he found his brother Thomas waiting for him with news to report. Arun had told him that after Harry's ship left port, the two of them would spend the night at the home of one of the captain's relatives. This was a great honor, and Thomas was looking forward to it.

Harry confided to Thomas how he had been feeling since leaving his father's office earlier in the day. "It's as if I were already on my way, Thomas," he admitted.

"I think perhaps you are dreading your good-byes, Harry. I know I would feel that way if it were I who was leaving and did not know when, if ever, I would see any of my family again."

"You are absolutely right, Thomas. As excited as I am about all that lies ahead, I do dread saying good-bye to…to…to all of you. I shall miss all of you terribly. I am glad I shan't have to take leave of you, at least, until we are actually at the ship, but how shall I get through the ordeal? How can I say good-bye to Father and Mother and all the others without bursting into tears?"

"You'll do fine, Harry. You always do. And if I see you about to bawl, I'll think of something to distract you."

"You mean like lunging at me and knocking me to the floor as you did yesterday?" He clapped his brother on the shoulder. "Ah, Thomas, you can always make me feel better. Let's go to dinner now and then spend the evening figuring out how to spend tomorrow."

"That's a lot of spending, Harry. You must suddenly be rich."

"Oh, you are getting to be a first-class tease, Thomas. Now let's go."

Harry needn't have worried about what to do on his last day at home. Lady Frankland took care of that quite thoroughly, constantly asking if he had remembered one item after another, giving him motherly suggestions concerning his behavior on board the ship, on his expeditions ashore, and when he finally arrived at Thirsk. She took him around to visit her friends so that they might offer their own advice along with their good wishes for a safe and peaceful voyage. By the time she finished with him, it was once again dinner time.

The cooks had prepared Harry's favorite dishes, and while he didn't have his usual hearty appetite, he ate a bit of each dish they put in front of him, thanking the servants profusely. Then the hour he dreaded was at hand. As his nine siblings prepared to go to bed, he shook hands soberly with each brother and kissed each of his sisters on their cheeks. Perhaps it was a good thing that his little sister Annie, of whom Harry was particularly fond, was one of the first to leave. Had she been last, he might never have been able to let her go. When it was time for Harry and Thomas to retire to their room for the night, Sir Henry shook Harry's hand with such vigor that it hurt, but Harry would not let his father know and allowed the gesture to continue as long as Sir Henry wished it.

Nothing Thomas could do for him would prevent a few tears from falling when it came time to give his mother a final embrace. Tears rolled down her cheeks, as well, and she did nothing to stop them. She smiled through them and asked, "What mother would not shed a tear or two on saying farewell to her beloved first-born son?"

The good-byes came to an end at last, and Harry and Thomas headed for their room, knowing Arun had set an unusually early wake-up time for them. They whispered beneath the sheets until both became drowsy and fell asleep. It was a toss-up which boy slept the most fitfully, yet neither was at all reluctant to get up and dressed for the long ride to the ship when Arun entered their room and told them it was time to go. Arun was waiting by the carriage for them when they left the house after eating what breakfast they could get down.

"Ah, Master Harry and Master Thomas, we have been blessed with a beautiful day for our journey," he told them. "I have tied your trunk to the back of the coach, and the horses are hitched up and ready to go. Shall we get started?"

"By all means," the boys replied simultaneously as they climbed onto the driver's seat beside Arun. They were off. Harry couldn't decide whether to take one last look behind him at the only home he had ever known. It might make him cry, and he didn't want to jump from the coach and beg his parents to let him stay in India. He reminded himself that a great adventure lay before him. Seconds before it would have been too late to look, he turned. "Good-bye", he whispered so softly that the others did not hear him. The coach turned a corner, and he headed for the next phase of his life.

Once they left the area with which the boys were familiar, Arun began to tell them about each new place they reached, answering their questions patiently and thoroughly. In a few hours they stopped by a clear stream to eat the lunch of bread and cheese and fruit that Arun had packed for them. They scooped up cupfuls of water to drink before using the stream as a wash basin for their hands. Arun told them the stream ran into the Hooghly River, which in turn ran into the Bay of Bengal. Harry found himself trembling as he realized how near they were getting to the end of this part of the journey and this part of his life. He turned to Arun and asked him to tell his Elephant Roundup story one last time. Arun understood the feelings his young charge was experiencing and began the familiar recitation. He told how he and his brother Anil had brought goats' milk to their mother while she was patting out dough for the flat bread called chappatis, which they would have for dinner. It was then that Uncle Arjan told them they would be in the khedda. Their jobs would be to help the elephant keeper, the mahout. They would feed and bathe the kumkies, tame elephants that were trained to help round up the wild herd. Arun and Anil would be called khotals. The two boys were excited. This was the first time they had taken part in a khedda.

At that time there were thousands of wild elephants in India. Most of the time they stayed deep in the jungle, but if food was scarce, they would come into a nearby village and smash everything in sight, eating the sugar cane and rice crops the people of the village depended on for their living. It was the custom in each village to send out hunters called yajamans to look for herds of the huge beasts, so that they could warn the village if it looked like trouble coming their way. The yajamans of Arun's village had spotted a herd working their way nearer to their huts and knew it was time to plan a khedda.

"Tell me about building the stockade," Harry begged. He could imagine the kumkies hauling huge teak logs, some as long as twenty feet in length, along with thousands of bamboo stems, and dropping them into the holes the men dug with their long-handled shovels. "Don't forget the ditches, Uncle Arun," he prompted. He knew the big beasts could easily knock down the fence if they wanted to, so the workers dug ditches around the stockade. Elephants can't jump and are afraid of falling down, so they would not try to cross the ditches which, like the roundup itself, were called kheddas.

Arun began to tell the boys about the shower bath system the workers rigged up for the elephants. Harry and Thomas laughed at the idea of a big kumkie taking a bath. The workers arranged sprinkler pipes in the branches of the trees and installed pumps at the river to provide the water. "Did you really wash those big elephants?" Harry asked. He still, after all these tellings of the story, wondered if Arun may have been teasing him. He wished he could have been there to watch.

"I most certainly did," the old man answered with feigned indignity. "Then we all went to the ceremony at the shrine of Mastiamma, Goddess of the Forest." The Indian people had ceremonies for everything, but this one was brief, and soon the khotals, mahouts and kumkies were on their way.

Arun was excited when he and Anil saw rows of fire on either side of the wild elephant herd. They were miles long and had to be tended day and night to keep the big animals from getting away. The boys knew elephants would not cross a barrier of fire.

Harry and Thomas were wriggling with excitement now. They knew the best part of the story was coming next. Arun continued, "We heard shouting, yelling, bamboo sticks hitting against each other, even the firing of shotguns, and we knew the drive was on in earnest. Anil and I rode our kumkies up as close to the wild elephants as we dared and herded them toward the stockade. We were so proud to be taking part in this exciting event. Everything was going smoothly when suddenly I heard Anil scream. A wild bull elephant was lumbering toward his kumkie with his head down and his tusks pointed right at Anil. I tell you, boys, that was one scared khotal."

"What happened then?" Harry asked, although he had heard the story many times.

"Well, sir," Arun went on, "I was following right behind Anil, and I saw a big old mango tree up ahead. I shouted to Anil to grab onto the overhanging branch. He barely caught hold of the limb in time. He scurried up that mango tree like a scared cat. I turned my kumkie around and went for help, praying all the time that the bull elephant would not knock down the mango tree with Anil in it. Poor Anil shivered up there in the tree for a long time, but finally the mahouts got the wild elephant back on the right track and went to rescue him. He was one relieved boy, I can tell you."

"I want to hear about crossing the river and all the fires," Thomas said. Arun smiled, remembering once again the two rows of bamboo rafts strung across the river on each side of the crossing area. Fires blazed on each raft to keep the wild elephants in line, and Uncle Arjan's huge kumkie stood in the river as an added assurance that the others would not escape and damage the village.

"Now tell us about Nabob and Rajah," Harry pleaded. He remembered that after the last elephants were safely in the stockade, and ropes were tied around their legs and necks, they were led to the peel khanna where they would be trained to work. Arun and Anil were assigned two young bull elephants to care for and promptly named them Nabob and Rajah.

"Which one ate the sugar off your hand, Uncle Arun?" Harry asked. Arun reminded him that had been Rajah's trick. Nabob spent most of his time splashing in the river.

As Arun finished his story, the coach arrived at the dock, and he immediately began his search among the many vendors to find the furniture Harry would need in his cabin. Harry and Thomas watched in awe as the Indian bargained with the sellers. He would tell them they were asking too much, and if they did not immediately come down in their price, he would walk away, only to be called back because the vendor had found some small reason to reconsider the amount.

Perhaps the desk had a small scratch or the wash basin showed a tiny crack in the rim. The candle seller reduced his price because he said he hadn't realized at first just how many the Indian was buying. It was a game played over and over on the docks. Each vendor had to save face the best he could, yet still get a fair price for his merchandise. Arun had done this before and knew to the penny the true value of each piece and refused to pay any more. When he had everything Harry would need, he offered two scruffy-looking men a bit more than the usual pay for the job, and quickly secured their services in loading the furniture onto the ship Harry would soon be boarding.

Thomas was spellbound at the sight of the largest vessel by far that either boy had ever seen. It was, of course, a Dutch East Indiaman. Such vessels had been making trips to and from England, India and the Orient since the sixteenth century, trading tea, raw silk, porcelain, silver, opium, and many other valuable cargoes.

"It's so big, Harry," Thomas said in wonder.

"Arun said it probably weighs something over 400 tons, Thomas."

"Four hundred tons, why that's as big as a hundred elephants."

"Give or take a few, Thomas. Come, let's go nearer to it and watch all the activity."

"Yes, let's. But what is Uncle Arun doing with all those cleats and staples and ropes and hammers?"

"He and his helpers will be securing my things in the cabin," Harry told him. "Otherwise, they would slide around during windy weather and might be severely damaged."

"They might even damage you, Harry, and I don't just mean your dignity."

"How shall I get along without you and your teasing?" Harry asked.

"Oh, you'll manage," Thomas replied, "but who are those awful-looking men over there? They are filthy and ragged, and they look as if they haven't had a good meal in a month."

"Arun said they are looking for jobs on board the ship. He said it is a hard lot for anyone, so it is mostly desperate men who take those jobs—derelicts, drunks, peasants, and sometimes even criminals."

"How can the captain trust this sort of crew to do the work properly, Harry? Wouldn't they be likely to be lazy or troublesome?"

"He must be very stern with them. Father told me that some captains threaten to beat these men or withhold their food and water at the least sign of trouble. Did you know the men might stay on the same ship for as long as two years without going to their homes? Uncle Arun said some of them will die at sea. Ships of this sort are the last choice of the crews. Most men prefer to work on fishing vessels or those which only travel routes that stay close to Europe. Father said the conditions on those ships may be even worse than on an East Indiaman, but the voyages are shorter and the climate more agreeable."

"I wouldn't want to take on such a job, would you?"

"Not at all. Uncle Arun told me that sometimes, especially when it comes to Dutch ships, the men are lured to the jobs with false promises, and if they are signed on well before the ship is due to sail, they are kept in the most awful conditions until that day."

"How terrible! Are you sure you'll be safe on this ship, Harry?"

Harry assured his brother that any disturbances were among the crew alone and would be taken care of quickly by the Captain and his officers. Thomas hoped with all his heart that Harry's assessment of the situation was true. "Do you think we can take a look at your cabin now?" he asked to change the subject.

"Here comes Uncle Arun, we'll ask him."

Arun signalled to the boys to join him and said he had completed the job of securing everything in the cabin. The three of them went aboard the huge vessel. "Your cabin is back here, Master Harry," Arun told him. Harry closed his eyes for a moment before taking his first look at the room which was to be his home for the next few months.

"You have done an excellent job, Uncle Arun, and please do not think I am ungrateful either to you or to Father, but it is not quite like the accommodations I have been used to at home."

"You have been most fortunate, Master Harry, but keep in mind that this is the very best accommodation offered. Look, you have a fine window to let in light and air. You will appreciate what you have more as the journey goes on. There are other passengers who would be very happy to exchange accommodations with you. I once was assigned to the steerage section, and, believe me, you would not want to be there. It is dark, dirty and smells terrible."

"Truly, Uncle Arun, I did not mean to complain. I was simply comparing the room to the spacious one I share at home with Thomas. Father told me about the different accommodations, and I am grateful to have this one. Truly I am."

"I know, Master Harry. Forgive me if I was too hard on you. I did not intend to be. But now I am afraid it is time for Master Thomas and myself to leave you. The bosun will soon be piping 'topmen aloft', which is the signal for the pilot to begin your journey out to the Bay of Bengal. Let me remind you once more of some things you must do. Be sure to get your bill of quarter and always salute the captain and officers whenever you see them on the quarterdeck." He looked into Harry's eyes and added, "I wish you the best possible voyage, Master Harry. Now, Master Thomas, we really must leave or we may well find ourselves in Thirsk with Harry."

"That would make me very happy, Uncle Arun. Perhaps you could stow away."

"I think Sir Henry would not appreciate that." The Indian paused. "Master Harry, may I take a liberty that is not usually mine?"

"What is it, Uncle Arun?"

"You have been like a son to me, and I would very much like to give you a fatherly embrace as you go on to your new life."

"And I would be pleased to receive it.," Harry told the old man. The two embraced, and Harry was startled to see tears in the eyes of the servant who had always kept a respectful and reserved distance from him. He was not, however, surprised to know that Arun had a deep affection for him, and he hoped Arun knew it was returned in kind.

Harry turned to his brother. "Now, I guess it's our turn, Thomas. I trust at this moment neither of us will feel the need for teasing the other. I shall write to you often and hope you will do likewise. Someone gave me a little hint about receiving letters which doubtless will have taken months to travel from the writer. He said it made it easier for him if he pretended they had been written just a few days earlier. I plan to follow his advice."

"I shall do that, too," Thomas replied. The boys' handshake quickly turned into a brotherly hug. Thomas and Arun left, looking back at Harry until they could no longer see him.

Harry heard the high-pitched sound of the bosun's pipe and the increased roar from the people on the dock. The sails were raised, and a brisk wind soon filled them. Whatever lay ahead, he was on his way to meet it.

CHAPTER 2

▼

As he waited for the ship's bell to summon the passengers to dinner, Harry thought of the family he had left behind. He was grateful that his father had prepared him so well for this voyage during that unusual time when he had Sir Henry's undivided attention. He wished he had been closer to his father, but as Governor of the British East India Company in Bengal, Sir Henry's days were filled with business, but Harry had no doubt that Sir Henry cared for him and his other children. He thought back to his twelfth birthday, which now seemed so long ago. The planning and effort his father put into that celebration was certainly proof of his affection for his oldest son.

It was May 10th in the year 1728. On that bright day in Bengal, Harry was not thinking about leaving India. His only concern was whether or not he would feel well enough to enjoy the birthday festivities that his father had planned. With Sir Henry's connections, it would no doubt be a spectacular show.

Harry was heartbroken when he awoke with a thumping headache and alternated between chills and high fever. The doctor was called and gave him some evil-tasting drink. Harry gagged and retched when he tried to swallow it, finally resorting to holding his nose and downing it in one great gulp. His body shuddered as he put down the cup. The doctor said he should stay in bed in the room he shared with his brother Thomas. Harry was feeling too sick to do otherwise.

"Uncle" Arun stayed with the boy and waved palm leaves over him to keep him comfortable. Harry slept fitfully for several hours, then at late morning Arun saw perspiration on the boy's brow. The sheets on his bed were soaked, and Arun called one of the women servants to change them. When they finished and Harry was once again dry and comfortable, Arun asked, "How are you feeling, Master

Harry?" Harry looked around the room and although shades had been drawn all around, he could tell it was still light outside.

"Much better, but still a little tired, thank you," he replied, then added wistfully, "Have I missed my birthday?"

"No, Master Harry, the festivities have not yet begun," the Indian told him. Harry wanted to get out of bed immediately, but Arun thought he should rest a little longer.

After another hour or more of sleep Harry pulled himself up to a sitting position, and feeling much stronger, asked Arun to send for his mother. Lady Frankland, an attractive woman, despite having given birth to seven sons and three daughters, entered the room a few minutes later. Her jet black hair was piled high on her head, making her appear taller than her five-foot-two-inch height. She wore an afternoon dress of blue and grey striped taffeta, which brought out the deep blue of her eyes. She had added a few pounds with each baby, but when she pouted over that fact, Sir Henry had gallantly replied, "That just means there is more of you I can adore, my darling." Lady Frankland never worried on that score again. Now she hurried to her son's bed. "Are you really better, dear?" she asked. "We were so worried."

"Yes, Mother, I feel quite well now. May I attend the birthday festivities?" Lady Frankland thought he could. She spoke to Arun, "Please get Harry's outfit and help him dress. Then we would be obliged if you would accompany him to the plaza and be sure he finds a shaded spot to sit in."

Arun nodded and mumbled, "Milady," and went to assemble Harry's clothing. He chose a fine embroidered lawn shirt, tan linen kneepants, cotton stockings and brown buckle shoes.

Harry told the old man, "Uncle Arun, I won't forget you when I leave for England. You're my very best friend. You have been with me for as long as I can remember, and you have taught me so many things. What shall I do without you?"

The old man was pleased but simply replied, "Come along now if you are to see all the sights."

Sir Henry had gone to great lengths to plan a special celebration for his oldest son's last birthday with his family. He had learned that some members of Britain's royal family would be coming to Bengal the next week and that Col. Wharton was planning a regimental parade as well as a rifle drill team exhibition to entertain them. Sir Henry arranged that Col. Wharton's dress rehearsal would be part of Harry's birthday entertainment as well.

Arun found the boy a seat on the plaza in the shade of an old mango tree. "I hear drums, Master Harry. I think you recovered just in time," he said. Soon Thomas came running over to sit beside his brother. The two boys watched excitedly as the regiment marched into the plaza, resplendent in their red jackets and tall furred headpieces. Harry thought they must be hot in those uniforms, but he was thrilled at the sight of them. "Just think," he said softly to Thomas, "they're here for me." The unit performed various intricate marching patterns that brought loud applause from the guests. Everyone cheered as they marched off. It had been a fine show.

Next came the rifle drill team. Harry had seen such an exhibition just once before, when he was six, and had never forgotten it. The eight men chosen for this honor performed a precision rifle drill without prompting. The crowd was awed when eight rifles, complete with bayonets, were flung high in the air. All were caught at the same time and the drill continued with none of the men missing a beat. The finale was the mirror drill. One of the eight soldiers was selected to be the leader. He marched back and forth in front of the seven others, stopping at last to face the man he had chosen to be his partner. He began another series of difficult moves with his rifle, and it was the duty of the other soldier to mirror those moves with his own rifle. This was all done at a fast pace and in silence. Harry and Thomas were filled with admiration as they watched the precise execution of the maneuvers.

Following that display were games and races for the children of Sir Henry's associates and others who had been invited to Harry's party. Harry wanted to join in the fun but was persuaded he shouldn't get too tired if he wanted to stay up for the fireworks which would begin when it got dark. He was allowed to partake of the goodies spread out on long tables. There were sandwiches, both dainty and hearty, cookies, fruits, cakes and cool fruit drinks.

The fireworks display over the reflecting pool in the plaza went on for nearly one half hour. The crowd oohed and aahed as one lovely shower of light and color followed another. Little children cried when particularly loud fireworks burst forth, but Harry and Thomas liked those best of all. When the display ended, Harry found his father and thanked him. "Father, it has been a wonderful birthday and one I shall never forget."

"Well deserved, I might add, Harry. You're a son to make any man proud." Sir Henry told him as he tousled his son's hair.

Harry went to bed with thoughts of the day's activities in his head. Soon they turned to imagining Great Thirkleby Hall at Thirsk in the North Riding of Yorkshire, far away in England, the homeland he would be seeing for the first time in a few more months.

CHAPTER 3

▼

A few days later, having completely recovered from the illness that nearly kept him from enjoying his birthday celebration, Harry was reading in the gazebo where his younger sister, Ann, was playing with her dolls. As she dressed them in their finest gowns, he could hear her talking to them, telling them of the lavish parties and other festive occasions they would enjoy when they were grown. She described their engagement parties and weddings, the beautiful gowns they would wear at those times, the food, the flowers, the music. Without warning, Ann lay down the beautifully dressed dolls and rushed over to Harry, climbed onto his lap and flung her little arms around his neck. "When I grow up, I'm going to marry you, Harry," she told her surprised oldest brother.

"Dear little Annie," he replied, "A man cannot marry his sister no matter how much he loves her."

"Then I shall marry someone just like you or I will not marry at all," she told him, pouting prettily.

"Oh, I'm sure you will marry, Annie," he told her. "Let's hope we each find someone to marry that we can love as much as we love each other."

"We will," Annie replied and went back to her dolls.

Just then Arun came loping across the lawn towards the gazebo. He stopped to catch his breath and said, "Master Harry, your father would like you to come to his private office right away." Harry patted Annie's head gently and followed Arun to the house, where he found Sir Henry waiting for him.

"Come in, Son. Thank you for coming so quickly. I had a few moments before my next appointment, and I have several things on my mind which I must tell you about. Have a seat. That one, over there, where I can have a good look at you while I speak."

When Harry was comfortably seated, Sir Henry began, "Now, Harry, you will be leaving Bengal soon. I suppose you are thinking sad thoughts about leaving the only home you have ever known and especially your brothers and sisters. I have noticed you appear particularly fond of your next brother, Thomas, and little Ann."

"Yes, sir, I am. Thomas and I have been good friends all our lives, and Annie is so sweet, who could help loving her?"

"Yes, yes. Your mother says the same thing about our daughter. She is a charmer. Sometimes I think too much so, but that's not what I brought you here for. No, there are things I must explain about your upcoming voyage. First, though, I would not want you to think you are being sent away as any sort of punishment for some wrong-doing you may have committed. Nor would I wish you to think we don't want to have you with us any longer. That is not the case at all."

"I have not thought those things, Father. I have often seen boys of my age in other families go off as I am about to do. I'm sure I am being sent for the best of reasons."

"I'm glad you understand that, Harry. Now you must also understand that there are many new experiences awaiting you. Some of these will be extremely satisfying, while others may seem frightening, silly, and unnecessary. They will certainly run the gamut. That's the way life is for all of us. However, I can assure you, you will one day be grateful for all these experiences, no matter of what ilk they are. I'd like to begin by telling you all I know about the journey you will soon embark upon." He pulled his pocket watch out of his vest, checked the time, returned it, and once more took up his remarks. "As you well know, I made the trip you are about to take but in the opposite direction some years back. Of course, I was not alone when I made it. My dear wife, your mother, was with me, which made every part of the journey more pleasant. Now, the ship you will voyage on is one of the class of ships known as the East Indiamen. I'm sure you saw one in the Bengal Bay once, but you were much younger at the time and may not recall it. These vessels are, of course, owned and operated by the East India Company in whose employ I have been since before my arrival here. These vessels have three purposes. They are first and foremost cargo ships, carrying goods from port to port, sometimes from as far away as the Orient. You may watch them unload tea or spices or silks at one port and load up again with whatever merchandise the people of that port area have to sell at the next port. Some of the best ships are those made by the Dutch, since they have managed to harness the power generated by their windmills, and their saws take less manpower to cut through the huge logs it takes to build such large ships. The cuts are more accurate as well. The Dutch also pride themselves on making sure every part and fitting is accurately made, so that it does it's job efficiently. You will be on a Dutch-made vessel, and the Captain is also Dutch. His name is Captain VanVleet. As is the custom, I went to his office in Bengal some months ago to interview him and make arrangements for your journey. I found Captain VanVleet to be a most personable man with more than the usual sympathy towards his passengers and his crew. You will find such character adds immeasurably to the comfort of your journey. Captain VanVleet was a guest at our home soon after we first met. Perhaps you recall seeing him here. He is a tall man with blue eyes and a long, graying beard and a rather loud voice. He is a man of great experience and has sailed in every kind of weather and every kind of sea with a minimum loss of life. I trust my perception of the man to be correct. I would not want you on a ship with one of those captains who are interested only in the profits they may earn and show little concern for others on board their vessels. Some of these are unbelievably corrupt, cruel and heartless, especially where their crewmen are concerned. They have been known to mete out floggings, keel haulings and even death to those poor sailors who commit even the smallest of sins. I've heard of men losing their lives because they complained about the quality of the food given them. Another who did not complain but tossed his rancid food overboard rather than eat it was severely punished for the act." Sir Henry noticed Harry's eyes had opened very wide. "Well, enough of that. It is not my purpose to frighten you, but merely to enlighten you. I'm sure you will be served quite palatable food, so there will be no need to whip you or throw you overboard." He tousled Harry's hair to show him this last was a joke.

"I appreciate what you are telling me, Father. I know very little about life on board any ship," Harry told him.

His father continued. "As I mentioned, there are three purposes for an East Indiaman. The second, as you no doubt have figured out, is to carry passengers. The third is to be well armed in case of attack by marauders, pirates or ships from other nations. Some of these scoundrels are looking to capture the ship itself, while most are interested primarily in the cargo. They can make a great deal of money selling stolen goods, and there are plenty of immoral men trying to do just that."

Harry stopped listening to his father's voice. He was imagining what it would be like to be attacked by pirates. He thought it would be exciting but at the same time very frightening. Sir Henry, noting the far-off look in his son's eyes, paused to gather up his thoughts before continuing.

"To get back to your accommodations on board. I have secured for you a cabin in the roundhouse, Harry. These are the most expensive cabins, and I trust you will find reason to be grateful that I have chosen one for you. The most pleasing aspect of the roundhouse cabins is that each has a window to let in fresh air and light. The one drawback to these cabins is that they are situated well to the stern under the poop deck. This means you will hear the pounding of the sailors' feet over your head. You must learn to ignore this distraction as soon as you can. You will find that other passengers in the roundhouse cabins are generally other high-born gentlemen and ladies who are travelling alone. By being in that area, these women can be protected to some extent by the captain, and they will enjoy more privacy than those in lower-cost cabins. Another advantage of the round-house is its convenience to the cuddy." Seeing a look on Harry's face that indicated he was unfamiliar with that term, he explained. "The cuddy is a large section of the ship which is usually divided into two parts. On one side is the captain's stateroom, while the dining room is situated in the other side. Beneath the roundhouse are housed gentlemen who could not afford the roundhouse, as well as unmarried army officers travelling on official business." Harry was once again listening intently.

"By far the most miserable accommodations are those in steerage. There is neither light nor air in steerage, and absolutely no privacy. After a few weeks in that hell-hole, breathing in the awful smells of unwashed bodies and worse, passing from one to another any diseases or germs some may have brought aboard, there may well be deaths occurring. Here again I have the word of Captain VanVleet that if such happens, he will treat each corpse with as much dignity as he can muster. It is his custom, he informed me, to wrap the deceased in a sheet, tie two cannon balls to the person's head and foot so that the body will sink quickly, and, before consigning it to the sea, he says a prayer over the dearly departed's soul. Some less sympathetic captains have been known to simply have a crew member toss the body over the rail with no ceremony. Then the passengers may be exposed to the unpleasant sight of seeing a dead body rolling about on the waves. I should not want to have you witness such a scene." Again he paused, then continued. "On either side of the steerage section are the cabins of the ship's officers. These are not grand, but they do have a porthole to provide light and some air. Any questions, so far, Harry?"

"Steerage sounds horrible. I'm glad I'll be in the roundhouse, but, Father, I am wondering how my cabin will be furnished."

"It is up to each passenger to furnish his own room. One reserves only the space on these vessels. I have arranged for Arun to purchase and to put into your cabin a daybed which will convert to a sleeping bed at night, a writing desk, a washstand with basin and pitcher, and two chairs. One of these will be a straight chair for use at your desk. The other will be a rocking chair, which I trust you will use when reading or even napping. He'll see to it that you have several candle-sticks and a goodly supply of candles. I trust he will also be able to find a small bookcase, and I have taken the liberty of ordering books for you. Am I correct in my understanding that you enjoy the works of Mr. William Shakespeare?"

"Yes, Sir, very much. I find his plays most interesting."

"Fine. I have ordered two of his most popular plays, *Hamlet* and *MacBeth* as well as all his plays about English kings, and a few of his lighter works, such as *Much Ado About Nothing* and *A Midsummer Night's Dream*. I have also chosen a few examples of more current literature. You, of course, may take with you any of your belongings from your room here in Bengal, including your clothing and a few keepsakes and whatever you think will help you while away the time on board."

"You have been most generous, Father. I am already feeling much better about leaving. I shall still miss all of you terribly, but I now see that there is much to look forward to in the future."

"Ah, Harry, you have no idea of all that lies ahead." Sir Henry himself had a faraway look on his face as he remembered some of the more exciting events of his own life. "I have just two more things to tell you about as far as the trip itself is concerned, and then I shall release you so that you may spend as much time as possible these last few days with your mother and your siblings."

"What are they, Father?"

"When you first board the ship, you will be given copies of the quarter bill. This is basically a list of rules and regulations governing your behavior on board. I urge you to study this carefully, as compliance with these rules will make your trip more pleasant, while noncompliance may well lead to extreme unpleasant-ness. Among the rules, you will find that you should salute before coming onto the quarter deck. This rule will be satisfied by merely touching your hat. You must never whistle on board this or any ship. Sailors are a superstitious lot and believe that whistling brings about many kinds of bad luck. It goes without say-ing that you are expected to be on time for meals. And lastly, each male passenger will be assigned an action station. You must be sure to memorize your station, and if given an order by the captain, you must obey it. This is all an effort to be prepared in case an unfriendly ship is spotted up ahead. I advise you to obey all orders given you in as manly and brave a manner as you can muster. This will not only bring you added respect from the crew but will insure that they have no cause to mistreat you after the danger has passed."

"I'll try to make you proud of me, Sir."

"I am proud of you, Harry, and I know you will give me no reason to change on that score."

"What is the final bit you wish to tell me, Father?"

"Ah, yes. As you know, you will be passing over the Equator on this voyage. Going from Bengal to England, you will come to that point fairly early on. As with all things, the celebration of this event varies from ship to ship. On some ships it can get very rowdy, even to the point of danger. Again, I believe Captain VanVleet will have the rite performed in a mostly entertaining manner. The worst I would expect of his presentation is some slight embarrassment. Should that occur, keep in mind that it will soon pass."

"What should I expect to happen at the Equator?"

"On Captain VanVleet's ship, you will likely see a sailor dressed as King Neptune who will make a big show of shaving the beards of the men who are crossing the Equator for the first time. He will doubtless use an over-size razor or even a sword or bayonet for this in order to add an element of anxiety to his performance. You, of course, have no beard, so will be spared that ordeal. It's probable also that the men will be dunked in water. I don't recall the significance of this, but it seems to be done on just about every ship. Captain VanVleet tells me this part of the ceremony is done in a large vat on his ship, and takes place in an atmosphere of fun. He does not believe in overly humiliating his passengers. He has known of cases on other ships where squabbling has resulted and even an occasional law suit has been filed by a passenger who feels he has been mistreated."

"I am eager to meet Captain VanVleet, Sir. He sounds like a real gentleman. I feel fortunate to be travelling on his vessel."

"I interviewed several captains before making my decision, Harry. Now, go on about your business. I'll have more to talk to you about tomorrow."

CHAPTER 4

▼

The next morning Harry and Thomas ate a hearty breakfast before walking over to the plaza where just a few days earlier they had watched British soldiers rehearsing for their performance before visiting royalty. "I want to fill my eyes with everything around here," Harry told his brother. "I don't want to forget anything, not ever. Thomas, has it occurred to you that we are English through and through, and yet we have never seen one foot of England's soil? We have lived our entire lives here in Bengal."

"I think of that often, Harry," Thomas admitted. "I envy your going to England, although I shall miss you very much."

"And I shall miss you, too, Thomas."

"Do you think Father will send me to Thirkleby when I reach the age of twelve?"

"I don't know, but I should be delighted if he does. Oh, we could have such fine times together there. Do you want me to ask Father when I see him this afternoon?"

Thomas thought for a moment before answering. "No, don't ask him. It would be too disappointing if he should say 'no'. If I don't know for sure, I can entertain myself with thoughts of what it will be like when I go. Does that make sense to you?"

"Yes, Thomas, it does. I often enjoy anticipating something even if it does not happen after all. Anyway, you can always ask Father if you change your mind."

"I would like to ask Father many things about England, but he is always so busy either at his office during the day or entertaining in the evenings. I rarely see him for more than a few minutes at a time."

"I know. At least being sent away has given me a little more time with him, and I have thoroughly enjoyed it. Of course Mother is always about. You could ask her to tell you about England."

"I have done so, but it always ends the same way with her telling me about fancy dress balls and high teas. Those are not the things I want to know about."

Harry understood, having endured Lady Frankland's enthusiastic monologs about aristocratic entertainment. "Thomas, if you will tell me what it is you wish to know more about, I shall try to get the information for you and will write you letters full of details."

"That would be fine, Harry, but truly I would most like to see these things for myself. I would give anything to see London. It must be an amazing place, and, of course, I am eager to know for myself what our home in Thirsk is like. I have read that some of the buildings in England are hundreds of years old. Hundreds! Can you imagine seeing them in real life, not just in pictures? That would be so wonderful! I understand there are great cathedrals and huge castles all over the country, and remnants of the Emperor Hadrian's wall and other Roman ruins. I would so like to see these things. Do write, Harry, but pray with me that I will some day get to see them for myself."

"I promise. Now, come with me and we'll walk around Bengal to see Father's factory one more time, and I want to watch the people, both the British and the Indian, in their daily routines."

Thomas had a new idea. "I wonder what kind of animals are native to England, Harry," he said.

"I don't know, but I doubt there are elephants and tigers in the forests there."

"Oh, Harry. I shall even miss being teased by you."

"And I shall miss having you to tease." Harry tousled Thomas's blond curls in a gesture of affection. "Hurry up, now. We only have a few hours before I must visit Father again in his study. I wonder what he will have to tell me today."

Promptly at one-thirty Harry knocked at his father's office door and was told to enter. "Good lad, Harry. You are right on time. That is an excellent habit to cultivate, Son. Everyone appreciates the person who respects them enough to be where they should be when they should be there, business acquaintances, friends, hostesses, everyone."

"I try always to be prompt, Father, and especially today when I am eager to hear what you have to tell me."

"Good, good. Since I told you about your impending voyage yesterday, I think today I shall speak more of what you may expect on arriving at your destination." He pursed his lips, remembering his last trip to England. "Your vessel will probably dock at Gravesend, which is some twenty miles downriver from London. It is an experience unlike any you have ever had, and it is important that you be prepared for it. In a word, Gravesend means chaos, at least it was that way when our ship was preparing to leave. I assume it is similar when a ship arrives. You will likely see baggage stacked by the hull of the ship, waiting to be picked up by departing passengers. There will be barrels and crates all around as well as farm animals which have been taken aboard at other ports. I have heard that some captains bring along whole packs of foxhounds when they sail. I suppose this is in case there is a foxhunt scheduled on shore when they arrive at any given port. The noise on the docks can be quite deafening with animals clucking, mooing, and oinking, the shrill sound of the bosun's pipe, coarse language and loud voices from crew members, and greetings from relatives come to get their loved ones. Despite the noise and confusion, I have no doubt you will find it all quite entertaining." Harry thought it would be an amazing sight.

"Your Uncle Thomas will be on hand to greet you and drive you by coach to Thirsk. If you so choose, you may sell the furniture you have used on the ship. There are always men around who buy furniture from arriving passengers and resell it to the next departing group. I understand a good profit can be made this way, since they manage to sell at a much higher price than that which they will give you. If you do not choose to sell these things, have Thomas arrange to have them shipped to Thirsk where you will no doubt find a place for them in one of the many rooms there."

"Oh, Father, you do make this all sound so exciting. I am more eager than ever to get started on this grand adventure."

"I am glad to see your enthusiasm, Lad. Now, I have a question for you? Do you know the difference between pride and vanity?"

"I believe they are very much alike, Sir, but it appears a good thing to have pride in one's country and perhaps in one's family, but it is vanity to be overly proud of yourself, your looks, your possessions, your abilities. Is that correct, Sir?"

"Close enough for our purposes today. I have waited until now to tell you a bit of your family history because I wanted to be sure you were mature enough to handle the knowledge wisely. I believe you are, and, in any case, it is right that you know who you are and where you come from, especially now that you will be living in England, where the Frankland family is held in high repute."

"I believe that is true here as well, Father."

"Thank you, Son. I have always tried to handle my business in a professional and honorable manner. What I will impart to you now is of more historical origins. Did you know you are a direct descendant of Lord Oliver Cromwell? You are, in fact, his great-grandson. Now there are some who would not be pleased to learn that and those who would be most gratified. In your case, it is true, and you may as well put the best light on it. Lord Cromwell led the Parliamentary forces against King Charles I almost one hundred years ago. That was the end of Charles's reign. Cromwell became the head man of Great Britain. Though he sat in the Coronation Chair and held a scepter and sword, as kings have traditionally done for many years, he declined the title of King and was known to all as Lord Protector. There are many who think he was the one who should have been protected against. In any event, he didn't last long. Lord Cromwell died in 1658, and by 1660 the monarchy was restored with the coronation of Charles II. It was that same year that Charles II conferred the title of baronet on William Frankland, your other great-grandfather. You should know that the name Frankland is very old and was given in feudal times to the original owner of the land. You may be wondering exactly how you are connected to Oliver Cromwell, Well, It was William Frankland's son Thomas, your grandfather and my father, who married the youngest granddaughter of Lord Cromwell, Elizabeth Russell, and that is the line of descendancy that connects you to him. Elizabeth Russell, my mother, was the daughter of Cromwell's youngest daughter Frances. It has been said that Frances was so attractive that King Charles II solicited her hand in marriage despite her father's part in interrupting the line of kings. You will notice that there are quite a few Elizabeths in our family, starting with your grandmother. Of course you know my wife was Elizabeth Cross, and your Uncle Thomas's first wife was also named Elizabeth, as is their daughter, your cousin Betty."

Harry wanted to know why he might not be pleased to be a descendant of Oliver Cromwell. "Well, Son, different people have different views of him as they do of most prominent people. In my opinion, Cromwell made religion a cloak to hide his ambition. He was, however, very clever at employing men of courage and capacity to do as he wished. He had his faults, like all of us, but no one can deny that he was one of the greatest generals England ever had."

"Then I shall be proud of my heritage," Harry declared.

Sir Henry smiled and said, "You might as well be. Now, I must get on with what I started to tell you, my boy. Your Uncle Thomas is the third baronet of Thirsk, and one day you will be the fourth, since Thomas has no male heirs, unless, of course, I outlive him, in which case I would become the fourth and you, as my oldest son, will be the fifth. Great Thirkleby Hall at Thirsk, for which you will soon be bound, is situated on the River Colleck and has been the family seat for generations. I believe you will find the Hall as beguiling as I have. Your mother and I lived at Mattersea before coming to India. I hope you will go there one day. It is well worth seeing. Now I have a gift for you."

"Oh, Father, you have given me so much already. I can never thank you enough."

"Perhaps the word 'gift' was misused. What I am giving you is something that is rightfully yours anyway, or will be when you become baronet." Sir Henry passed over to young Harry the Frankland coat of arms mounted on a beautifully carved mahogany plaque.

"It's beautiful! I shall cherish it all my days. I shall study it when I get back to my room. Look at the lovely blue dolphins, the wreath, the anchor. Thank you."

Sir Henry was pleased by his son's enthusiasm. "Have you noticed the family motto?" he asked.

"I have seen it before. Libera terra: liberque animus."

"Do you know what that means, Harry?"

"I believe you once told me it means 'Free soil and free soul.'"

"Well done, son. I trust you will find a space to hang it in your room at Thirsk."

"Proudly, Father."

"Well, since I have a meeting scheduled at three, we must get on with those things I want to tell you. I have requested that your Uncle Thomas, if he can take the time, show you some of your homeland rather than going directly to Thirsk. If he cannot oblige me in this, then you must make a point of going around at a later time. Among the sights I would hope you can see are Hampton Court, home of King Henry, the eighth. I believe, but I would have to look it up to be sure. That's a course of study you would be well advised to undertake, learning the order of kings and the history of our great homeland. There are so many grand and glorious places to visit that it would take me days to mention all of them, so I shall limit my list to only a few of the most outstanding. A great deal of building is going on in London these days, but of greater interest to me are the old places."

"I do hope Thomas can go there some day. He has a deep interest in architecture and would find it most exciting to see the places you speak of," Harry remarked.

"Well, of course Thomas will go there, and soon. He is but eighteen months younger than yourself, so I would expect to send him no later than two years hence."

"Oh, Father, may I tell him? He would be so pleased."

"Certainly, you may, Boy. It's no secret. But let us continue. I believe I have mentioned Hampton Court. A bit farther along you will come to Salisbury Plain and there you will see rising from the flat ground surrounding it a most magnificent cathedral named for the plain. This has long been my favorite of all the cathedrals because of its warm and mellow interior. The cathedral was started in the year 1220, more than five hundred years ago, and has the tallest spire in all of England, being over 400 feet in height. The grounds there are most beautiful, and you will see a medieval gateway as well as houses that are also from the thirteenth century. Inside you will find one of the remaining copies of the Magna Carta, which lists liberties King John was forced to assent to at Runnymede in 1215. It is well worth a look.

"Again, it is not far from Salisbury to a most peculiar sight. It is called Stonehenge and is thought to date back to 3000 B.C. There is much controversy about who built it and its purpose, but it is generally accepted that it represented some ancient religious sect. It consists mainly of a circle of huge stones standing upright with similar huge stones placed across the tops of them. Another mystery is where the stones came from and how those ancient people managed to haul them to their present location and lift the top stones in place. In time, perhaps, that mystery may be solved."

He continued, "You must not miss seeing Bath, where they have discovered ancient Roman baths which gave the place its name. Did you know the Romans first came to England before the birth of our Lord Jesus Christ? It is grand to know there are still remnants of them in existence today. My boy, I wish I could visit these places with you, the walled city of Chester, Stratford-on-Avon, home of your author friend Mr. William Shakespeare, Buckingham Palace in London, as well as Westminster Abbey, which was founded back in 1050 on the site of an even earlier church. Nearly all of England's kings have been crowned there, starting with the Saxon Harold in 1066, and many are buried there as well. My favorite of all is Windsor Castle out farther in the country, with its crenellated turrets. A lovely sight. The original castle was built on the spot by William the Conqueror and has been added to and remodeled many times since."

Harry was nearly breathless thinking of all these wonderful places he might soon be seeing for himself.

"But you must not think England is all cathedrals and castles," his father continued. "In London you will find the Tower of London begun by William the Conqueror in 1078 and still being added to today, and I have read that Sir Christopher Wren, who is nearly 90 years of age now, recently completed another great new building in the heart of London. That is St. Paul's Cathedral, finished just eighteen years ago. It stands where once stood churches of the Norman and Saxon people. But, I'm back on cathedrals again, aren't I? England has a great variety of everything, landscapes, weather, cultures. You should take one of your vacations in the lovely Cotswolds area where you will see everything from the mullion-windowed manor houses to thatched-roof village homes, arched bridges and Romanesque abbeys. It truly is a beautiful place to visit.

"Here I've rambled on and on and not yet mentioned the coastal portions of our beautiful homeland. The shores range from high cliffs, including the white cliffs of Dover, to sandy beaches where people of means enjoy their holidays. There are several great universities, also, Cambridge and Oxford being the most noteworthy. It is truly a marvelous country for one so small in size, and I shall consider it an important part of your education for you to see as much of it as you can.

"Ah, I see it is fast approaching the hour of three, and since I wish to practice what I preach about promptness regarding a meeting I have scheduled in just a few minutes, I shall excuse you now and request that you come here again tomorrow when I shall perhaps have further instructions for you and when I will hand over letters I should like to have delivered to family members and friends."

"I shall be happy to perform this service for you, Father. It is little enough in light of all you are doing and have done for me."

"Run along now, and don't forget to have a visit with your mother. You must spend as much time as possible with her before you go. I have observed that she is already beginning to miss you. I suspect a tearful farewell when you two part at last."

Harry would happily spend an hour with his mother, but first he must find Thomas and tell him that they will be reunited in Thirsk in no more than two years.

CHAPTER 5

▼

After searching for Thomas throughout the house and all over the grounds, Harry concluded his brother must have gone off to visit one of his friends. His news would have to wait a bit longer. For now, he would visit his mother. He found her on the veranda engaged in embroidering a table runner.

"Ah, Harry. I have been thinking about you for the last hour or more," she greeted him. It pained him to see a look of sadness cross her pretty face. He knew she did not want to face the fact that he was leaving soon.

Harry sat down beside her on the wide settee and prepared himself to listen to one of her nostalgic dissertations. He had judged her mood correctly, for she immediately began regaling him with stories about what a good infant he had been, what an adorable toddler, how bright he was at ages three and four. He resisted the urge to finish her sentences for her, although he could certainly do so, having heard these tales many times before and always in the same words. On this day, he didn't care what she spoke of, he was simply glad to have this time alone with her before he left for England. Who knew how long it might be before he saw his mother and all his family again? He felt a sad look cross his own face. He was now doubly glad that Thomas would be with him in two years.

Lady Frankland had been sewing her neat stitches all the time she spoke. She had arrived at a good stopping point now and told Harry he could go along since she had to see the cooks about dinner. "But I must hold you as often as I can these last hours you will be with me," she said, as she clasped him to her and kissed his forehead." Usually, now that he was twelve, he tried to avoid such expressions of affection from his mother, but knowing he might have few occasions to experience them again, he submitted without hesitation. He loved his mother dearly and the smell of her perfume, a blend of spices and sandalwood, would remind him of her and of India for his whole lifetime.

On leaving Lady Frankland, Harry came upon Thomas just entering the house. "Come with me to our room, Thomas," he urged. "I have news for you that I know you will be glad to hear."

"What is it, Harry?"

"I shall tell you when we get to our room." He had decided that was the most appropriate place to tell Thomas what their father had said. It was the room they had shared for several years, and they had had many comforting and confidential chats there.

Thomas nearly ran to the room and when they were both inside, closed the door against interruption by their other siblings. "Come on, Harry, what is it?"

"You must understand I kept my promise not to ask, but the information came about naturally when my conversation with Father came to the subject of architecture. I told him you would especially enjoy seeing the castles and cathedrals he wants me to visit, and he said that you would also see them when he sends you to Thirsk not more than two years hence."

"Oh, Harry, that is the best news I ever received." Without warning, he lunged at his brother and threw his arms around him in a spontaneous hug. The action caught Harry off guard, and the two boys fell to the floor in a tumble of arms and legs, with Thomas landing on top. He was the first to get up. "Are you hurt, Harry?"

"Only my dignity," Harry assured him. "However, I have one more piece of news for you and this time I believe I shall stay here on the floor when I tell it to you."

"That may be a good idea, since I would not wish to hurt your dignity twice in one day," his brother returned.

"Ah, Thomas, it seems you are beginning to catch onto the fine art of teasing at last. You may yet be my match. You must practice on Robert and Frederick while I'm gone!"

"I shall, you may count on it, but what is the other news?"

"Uncle Arun says you may come with us to the ship if you like. He will purchase furniture on the dock when we get there and will hire a helper to carry it onto the ship, so we have only to carry my personal belongings on our coach. Arun will tie my large trunk onto the rear of the coach, so there will be plenty of room for us inside, and he would welcome your company on the return trip. I hope you will agree to this, since knowing that you have seen my cabin will be a comfort to me if I succumb at times to homesickness."

"Of course, I'll come. Nothing could stop me. Oh, this is a day I shall remember all my life."

The two brothers chatted happily about all the things they would experience when they were reunited in Thirsk until it was time to get ready for their evening meal.

Harry once again arrived promptly at his father's office the following afternoon, wondering what interesting things he would hear this day. His father greeted him in his usual hearty manner and explained that he had planned to describe yet more sights Harry should see all over England and even some in Wales and Scotland. "But, since I have already whetted your appetite for such things, I have decided to leave it to you and your Uncle Thomas to plan these tours on your own. There is another subject which needs to be discussed, one I generally avoid, but in this case, it is necessary."

"What is it, Father?"

"That most necessary of oft-times evil things, money. As you know, you will be staying with your Uncle Thomas and his family at Great Thirkleby Hall. He has generously arranged for you to have use of a suite of rooms on the second floor, and you will take your meals with his family. I sent Thomas a sum of money to cover your first year there and will send a like sum each year you are with him. However, you will need some money for your own personal use. I also sent what I trust you will consider a generous amount, and he will pass it on to you as you need it. Since you have not had experience in handling finances, it would be wise if you consulted Thomas whenever you wish to purchase anything of significant cost. For the first years, you will have little expense, but as you get older and begin to receive invitations to dinner parties and balls, you will be obliged to bring gifts to your hostesses on each occasion. Thomas will advise you what is appropriate, although a bottle of good wine is always acceptable. There will be times when sending flowers is expected. And, of course, you will have to have appropriate clothing for these occasions. Later there will be social occasions with your peers that require certain expenditures."

"You have provided for every occasion it would seem, Father. It is true that I have had no dealings with money, but I am by nature rather cautious and have no doubt that with Uncle Thomas's advice I shall learn quickly to handle it well."

"My boy, I shall miss you. I have had so little opportunity to get to know you as well as a father should know his son. It would be a comfort to have you around these next few years, especially as I foresee changes coming in India and in the company I represent here."

"Really, Father. What are these changes?"

"They are for the most part political in nature, but political matters often become matters of conflict between nations. I hope we can avoid such conflicts, since they cause much misery and pain and usually end with things being pretty much as they might have been with successful negotiations between parties. Depending on what happens, it could even mean the end of the East India Company in India. That would be a profound disappointment to me to say nothing of my losing my job here. Are you aware that the company under one name or another has been here since the last day of the year 1600? The very factory in which I work here in Bengal was built in 1690. The company was founded strictly as a trading company, but in recent years has been more and more involved in politics and most recently appears to be acting as an agent of British imperialism. It is in this regard that I pray negotiations can be successful and war thus avoided."

"It seems strange that having been all my life in Bengal, with you as Governor of the East India Company factory here, I should be so ignorant of the company and its history. I believe I shall add that to my list of subjects in which to become better informed."

"Good Lad. Each time I speak with you I find myself more and more proud of you. Now go. Today and tomorrow are your last days here. You will be leaving on Friday to board your ship, which is scheduled to leave the harbor that evening, then on to the Bay of Bengal and your voyage to England, and I wish you a safe and pleasant journey."

CHAPTER 6

▼

Harry had finished reminiscing and writing in his journal when the passengers were summoned to dinner by a sailor beating "Roast Beef of Old England" on his drum. Dinner was served at 2 o'clock on this particular vessel, and all the ladies and gentlemen present were formally dressed. On this day, the seas were calm, so there was little danger of winds blowing out the cooking fire in the galley or tables and chairs flying around the dining room. As a precaution, long rolls of cloth were tied across the table between place settings to keep plates from sliding onto the passengers' laps, a particularly unpleasant experience when they were full of meat with gravy ladled over it. Harry soon understood that dinner at two was the main meal of the day and generally consisted of three courses, which varied from day to day.

For this first meal on board, there was a full complement of guests at the captain's table, the majority of the passengers having not yet succumbed to the seasickness which would soon overtake them. When they finished eating, the ladies left the dining room to read or embroider or write in their journals. The gentlemen stayed on to share a decanter of port which was passed around among them several times, Captain VanVleet being more generous than some of his fellow mariners. Spirited conversation went on until the captain rose to his feet, the signal for the men to leave. Harry, of course, left with the ladies, being too young to partake of the port.

The English custom of tea at 6 p.m. was observed on board ships of either English or Dutch origin. This was followed at 9 pm. by a light supper of soup, cheese, and slices of cold meat, after which the passengers retired to their cabins. Captain VanVleet had observed the "candles out by 10 o'clock" rule long before it became a requirement of law. This was necessary because East Indiamen captains customarily shortened sail at dusk, and travelling at a slow pace made them easy prey for pirates. With lights out, there was less likelihood of being seen by any marauders.

Harry was glad to have a few minutes to begin reading one of the plays by Shakespeare that his father had so thoughtfully provided. He opened his window just a crack to let in fresh air and promptly fell asleep with the play unread on his lap. Fortunately, he awoke in time to snuff out his candle and make up his bed for a proper night's rest. He had been afraid he'd be too keyed up to sleep, but that turned out not to be the case. He slept a deep and dream-free sleep.

At eight a.m., Harry was wakened by the bell which signalled the changing of the watch as well as the call to breakfast. He dressed quickly and ran to the dining room where he noticed there were fewer passengers at the table than he had seen the evening before. Captain VanVleet motioned to him from the head of his table. He invited Harry to sit beside him. Harry wondered why he was being given that honor. He felt sure it was because of his father that the Captain recognized him in this way, but seeing few others at the table, it could have been merely the Captain's desire for company. "Good morning, Master Harry," the captain greeted him in a hearty voice. "It appears you are one of few who are able to partake of our morning meal."

"Where are the others, Sir?" Harry asked.

"No doubt their stomachs vill not allow them to consider eating our fine fare of tea and biscuits, or the corned beef and tongue or even some porridge from the officers' table."

"My stomach is just a bit queasy, Sir, but I believe I can manage one of those delicious-looking biscuits and some tea."

"Those pretty biscuits appear better than they are, Lad. You vill find them very hard. Be careful or you might break one of your fine white teeth on one. I have heard it said that vere one to put one of our biscuits in a slingshot and let it fly, one could kill an albatross at twenty paces."

Harry was only convinced that the captain was not teasing him when he bit into one of the misleading biscuits. "Thought I vas pulling your leg, eh, Lad?" the captain asked, grinning widely. "I say, Master Harry, how vould you like to follow me around for the day? You could learn vat the captain does on a vessel like this, and I could show you many parts that most passengers never get to see."

"Thank you, Captain VanVleet, you do me a great honor, and I should be grateful for the opportunity you offer," Harry responded.

"Then if you are through trying to bite through that biscuit, let us be on our vay."

Scarcely daring to believe his good fortune, Harry left the cuddy with Captain VanVleet and headed for the main deck, where they would have an excellent view of the rigging and sails of the large vessel. The captain asked Harry if he had noticed the ornate decorations on the exterior of the ship when he was on the dock.

"Oh, yes, Sir. It is beautiful. I had not expected to see so much gold leaf and carved flowers nor the heraldic shield. It made me think of the shield my father gave me with the Frankland coat-of-arms on it. Would you like to see it sometime? I would be glad to show it to you if you are interested."

"I should be most interested, my boy. I found your father to be a very fine gentleman, indeed, and I have heard it said that he has been an excellent governor in Bengal for the English part of our East India Company. Perhaps you vill bring the coat-of-arms to the dinner table tonight. Did you notice the vindows of the stern and quarter galleries?"

"I was quite impressed by them, Sir. Everything about the ship is beautiful."

"It is that, but, Lad, sometimes looks are deceiving, just like our morning biscuits. To a true man of the sea, there are things about this ship which those who designed it could have done better. It could have been made more efficient. For instance, most merchant vessels are built to be three times as long as they are vide, but the East Indiamen, which need to be able to stow huge quantities of cargo, have been built too long, too narrow, and too deep, in my opinion. They are three-and-one-half times longer than they are vide. That may not seem like a big difference to you, but such dimensions do not make the vessel a good sailor."

"Why is that, Sir,?" Harry wanted to know.

"I vill tell you. Because of her shape, especially her rounded bottom, she can travel no more than three or four knots per hour in ideal sea conditions, which is but half the speed of today's varships, and vorse than that, in calm vaters ven she carries much weight, especially ballast, she gets as cranky as a sailor's vife and then she vallows and lurches and rolls around so that nearly everyone on board gets the seasickness. And vhen she sails close to the vind, she goes more sideways than forward, vhich only prolongs our journeys."

"What you said about the warships, Sir, would that not make our ship easy prey for them?"

"Ah, my boy, you catch on quickly. You are quite right, and even though ve carry plenty of cannon and guns, the arms must be stored in out-of-the-vay places because ve also carry so many passengers. It vould take us two hours to get them and be ready to defend ourselves. By then it vould probably be too late."

"Then we must pray we are not attacked."

"I pray that 24 hours a day, my boy. Now I must see that all my crew are busily engaged in their various occupations. It takes a good many men to run this vessel. You have already heard the bosun and his pipe. And the arms I mentioned do not shoot themselves, ve must carry one or more gunners aboard. Things can go wrong on shipboard just as they do in our homes, so we need to have carpenters, caulkers, joiners and coopers with us. And our meals do not cook themselves, so, of course, ve must hire cooks. And, since I could become disabled or incapacitated, there must be officers who could take my place to run the ship."

"My brother and I saw many men on the dock who were looking for jobs on this ship. They appeared to be a very motley group. My Uncle Arun said they were derelicts and drunks and worse."

"Your Uncle vas correct. They do like their grog, but we ration it or they vould be drunk all the time, and ve vould never get to our destinations. It takes a strong hand to keep these men under control and doing the jobs they need to do." He checked his watch. "I must beg your forgiveness, Harry, but I have some duties to attend to now, and I fear ve must call short our tour. Perhaps ve can pick it up another day. I vish you a fine day and that your stomach vill not get more queasy."

"Thank you, Captain. I have enjoyed this very much. I shall return to my cabin and write all I have seen in my journal. I would be glad to join you at any time."

So the days passed as the great ship made its way slowly across the Bay of Bengal. When they reached the Equator, Harry found his father's description of the expected ceremony to be quite accurate. Because of his age, and lack of a beard, he was spared King Neptune's close shaving, but he was not so fortunate when it came to the dunking. It was an unusually hot day, so he simply waited for his clothes to dry, as did most of the men who also were dunked.

Eventually came a cry from the crow's nest of 'Land Ho'. They were approaching their first stopping place, Johanna in the Comoro Islands off the east coast of Africa, between the continent and the island of Madagascar. Harry stood at the rail to watch nearly-naked islanders paddle their outrigger canoes out to meet the ship. They carried fresh fruits such as pineapples, bananas, and oranges, as well as fish, poultry and eggs. It was because of them that Harry and the other passengers were able to enjoy fine meals, at least until the supplies ran out, which more often than not occurred at some point in a months-long journey. Captain

VanVleet told Harry that they had been extremely fortunate not to have been involved in any unpleasantness so far, since there were so many pirates and privateers roaming the Bay, that not even the great British Navy could always protect them.

As the passengers became more used to the roll of the ship, and their stomachs returned to normal, at least temporarily, Harry realized they were beginning to form into small groups for cards and backgammon. On this particular ship there were only a few young, single women, but as always, they were much under the protective eye of Captain VanVleet, and any young men, or old ones, were well-advised to be very careful in approaching them. These women generally travelled with an older woman as chaperone, and she made every effort to keep them firmly in check. Some of the young men were engaged in learning a new language which would be necessary if they found positions with The East India Company or any company which regularly had commerce with such exotic countries as Portugal, Persia or Hindustan. Harry was content to stay pretty much by himself. He had his books and plays to read, his journal to complete, and Captain Van Vleet from time to time invited him to visit parts of the vessel he had not yet seen. He appeared to be the only young boy aboard, and he did not expect the adults to befriend him. He did, however, look forward to their visit to Capetown as they rounded the Cape of Good Hope. His father had told him that Cape Town was founded in 1652 as a Dutch East India Company supply post and that it was famous for its gold and emeralds.

Harry noticed the waves were getting higher, and the wind began to blow much harder. He could see crewmen rearranging sails in anticipation of a storm. This would be a new experience, but one he was not sure he was ready for. As the wind grew stronger, the vessel pitched violently, sending any unsecured furniture sliding back and forth across the cabins, and causing even the hardiest, including Harry, to suffer the misery of seasickness. Deciding that staying in his bed was the best idea, he began to pull off his shoes and stockings just as the ship pitched forward. He fell off the bed and bruised his shoulder. It took him several tries before he was able to lie on the bed, and he thanked Arun once more for having the foresight to position it so that it tipped forward and back rather than from side to side, which he learned was far worse. Although he hoped the stormy violence would soon end, it would be nearly forty-eight hours before the seas were once again calm.

Arriving at Cape Town, it was a relief to all to put their feet on solid ground again. The passengers would be staying overnight, most of them in the homes of Dutch families living there. These good people, long known for their cleanliness, provided excellent meals, and, best of all, they spoke English. While the ship took on supplies in Table Bay, the passengers enjoyed visits to the winery at Constantia and the majestic, flat-topped Table Mountain, which dominates the city. In the evening they attended dinner parties and dances. Harry sat on the sidelines, watching the dancers, until he felt tired enough to head for his cabin and bed.

Cape Town was situated approximately half way between Europe and Asia, and ships travelling in both directions met and exchanged news of the places they had come from. The Dutch called Cape Town "The Tavern of Two Seas". Harry was grateful that his father had provided him the opportunity to leave the ship. Not only would he enjoy the sights on land, but it would be a nice change to step once again on solid ground.

Back aboard, and with the weather now calm, Captain VanVleet once again invited Harry to spend time with him. He showed him a map of the whole Atlantic Ocean with the route the ship would take clearly marked out on it. Harry wondered why they would be heading toward the coast of South America on a trip to England, but he didn't like to ask. He assumed it was to avoid some sort of bad weather or an area in great danger from marauders. He saw that they would be stopping at the Canary and Madeira Islands to take on more drinking water, along with more fresh fruits and vegetables. They would also purchase quantities of a local wine which had become very popular with people living in India. Harry and the other passengers were glad to see the fruit and vegetables, since the supply was running low on board, and the boxes of greens and other vegetables the crew were trying to grow were not doing well.

The vessel had been at sea for nearly four months when they reached Lisbon, Portugal. They still had to cross the Bay of Biscay and enter the English Channel, and Harry was well aware that they could yet face two extremes of weather and sea conditions at any point along the ship's route. There might be too much wind, an event he had not enjoyed when he experienced it earlier, or too little wind, the doldrums, which could keep a sailing ship stuck in one spot for weeks at a time. Captain VanVleet, being an experienced mariner, chose a route that had the best chance of avoiding these misfortunes, but even the best planning could not assure they would miss them entirely. Harry saw that some passengers were becoming bored and a little testy. Perhaps, he thought, it is well I have not been too close with any of them. I should not like to be subjected to such sarcastic remarks as I have overheard among the passengers. He would continue to spend his time with Mr. Shakespeare's plays or writing in his journal.

Although long and often tedious, it had not been the worst of trips, and Harry had memories to last a lifetime, but he would be as happy as anyone when the great vessel pulled into port not far from London. He began packing his belongings long before the ship tied up to the dock. He hoped his Uncle Thomas was as prompt a man as his father and that they would recognize each other. One of the first things he would do when they reached Great Thirkleby Hall would be write a very long letter to his brother Thomas.

CHAPTER 7

▼

After four and one-half months at sea, the ship arrived at its destination, the dock at Gravesend. As there had been at its point of departure in India, there was once more general chaos all around. Again, groups of families and friends waiting to greet or say good-bye to arriving and departing passengers were shouting and waving. Vendors wishing to buy or sell furniture and other goods were calling out their intentions. Animals mooed, clucked, and barked, while seagulls squawked overhead, and arriving and departing vessels made themselves known with a cacophony of horn-blowing and whistles. Harry wondered how his Uncle Thomas would know when the ship was arriving; after all, every vessel at sea had to contend with storms, doldrums, and undependable winds, all of which could change their arrival date by several days or more. He also wondered how he would recognize his uncle. He had seen him once or twice when he was a toddler, but not in recent years, and both must have changed considerably.

To his great relief, he immediately spotted a man who looked much like his own father, and the man was carrying a sign on which was printed "Harry Frankland".

"That must be him," Harry thought and headed toward where the distinguished gentleman stood.

"Uncle Thomas?" he inquired politely.

"Ah, Harry, it is you. I think I would have picked you out from the crowd. You look like your father did when he was twelve, except he had light hair."

"Yes, Sir, I inherited my mother's black hair, as you can see. My brother, Thomas, your namesake, got Father's light hair and complexion."

"Well, Son, it's good to see you. I trust your trip was reasonably comfortable."

"Yes, Father was most generous in providing me with the best cabin available. May I inquire how you knew when we would be arriving, Uncle Thomas?"

"Rather by guess and by gorry with a bit of English luck thrown in, Lad. I had business in London last week and made several inquiries to learn if anyone had heard of your position. It seems a merchant vessel passed your ship off the coast of Portugal and estimated that without unexpected interruption, it should arrive here today. I had errands in London again today, and as you see, it worked out quite favorably. I took the liberty of sending two of my servants with a wagon to pick up your furniture and transport it to Thirkleby, unless, of course, you prefer to sell it here, in which case I'll instruct them to do that for you and then enjoy a day in London."

"I've given that matter much thought, Uncle Thomas, and if you think there is room for it at Thirkleby, I should like to take it there."

"It shall be done. Now, let's get to my coach and head to Yorkshire. Oh, I must beg your forgiveness. I know your father wished me to immediately take you on a tour of the area, but I have some pressing business to attend to and must get back to the Hall. We shall undertake our touring at a later date if that is satisfactory to you."

"Quite satisfactory, Sir. In the beginning I had looked forward to such touring. Father told me about a particularly interesting place called Stonehenge, and I truly hope to see it one day, but after such a long time on board the ship, I look forward even more to being in a house where the dinner table and chairs stay put, and my bed does not pitch and yaw all night long."

"I can well sympathise with you on that matter, being a navy man myself. So, it's off to Yorkshire, then." He signalled the two grey steeds to move forward, and they were on their way. "I'll see to it that you get to Stonehenge at the first opportunity. It really is remarkable and quite worth seeing. It seems to have grown out of a large field, but, of course, it was man-made. There is much mystery concerned with Stonehenge. We have yet to discover exactly who built it and why, although earlier this century a gentlemen by the name of John Aubrey came up with the idea that it was built by Druids as temples. I find that hard to believe, since what I've always heard about the Druids is that they held their celebrations in clearings in the forest. They say that the largest sandstone rocks, called sarsen, point roughly to where an observer standing in the center of the circle would see the sun rise on the longest day of the year. The first mention of Stonehenge in modern times was just 70 years after the Norman Conquest of England. You may think I use that word "modern" rather loosely, but it is believed that the original structure was built perhaps as much as 5,000 years ago. It is still unknown where they found the stone to build with, since the nearest stones of that type are at least ten or twenty miles from where Stonehenge is located. Another mystery is how they managed to get those huge stones up on top of each other. They must weigh several tons each."

"I hope they figure this out during my lifetime, Uncle. I also wonder what happened to the people who built Stonehenge," Harry said.

"That's another mystery, Harry. It could have been famine that wiped them out, or some plague. Perhaps some stronger group of raiders took them away. Another thought I have heard expressed occasionally is that it could have been a celibate group of worshippers, and with dwindling numbers joining them, they eventually died out. I, too, would like to know the answers to these questions."

Harry was pleased to find his uncle easy to talk with. They exchanged information about their families, and Thomas chuckled as he made an admiring remark about his older brother's large family. "My second wife Dinah and I have not been blessed with sons," he reported. "We have just two girls, Elizabeth, the apple of my eye, the daughter of my first wife, and Dinah, named for her mother, my second wife. She is near your age, perhaps a bit younger. Your Aunt Dinah is quite keen on meeting you, and you may expect to be mothered, if not smothered, by her.

As they drove along, Harry soon realized that his uncle had a sense of humor and would likely turn out to be somewhat of a tease as well. This made him feel comfortable in his uncle's company, and he looked forward to the next years with great pleasure. Soon Thomas broached the subject of Harry's education, the purpose of his journey to England. "I have lined up several excellent tutors and only await your choice of subjects before choosing the first ones. Have you given any thought to that matter, Harry?"

"Actually, Sir, I have. As you may know, my brother Thomas will be coming here in less than two years, and I thought it would be wise to postpone studying any foreign language until then, since I believe our studying together would be helpful to both of us. Since Thomas has a more mathematical bent than I, I should likely benefit from also sharing those studies with him. I promised Father I would study English history and learn the order of kings. Also, I have a lively interest in science, so that would be a course I look forward to eagerly. I don't know how many courses I should take on, so perhaps you can help me with that. If it is possible, I should like to study English literature as well as art and music quite thoroughly, perhaps some of each every year."

"Fine choices, Son. I have a particularly gifted history tutor in mind. In addition to English and world history in general, he can give you much information about our own area of Yorkshire. Since I want you to be free to travel with me from time to time, as I go about my duties as a Lord of the British Admiralty, I think four courses to start will be sufficient. I think your interest in English literature is quite admirable. Shall we start with the works of Mr. William Shakespeare?"

"I have read several of his plays. Father generously provided me with both historical plays and a few lighter ones for my reading aboard ship. In four months I was able to read all of them at least once, and some of them two or more times."

"Good, good. Then we will concentrate on some more recent authors, although I think you might enjoy conversations with your tutor about the plays you have already read. The Bard was a sly devil and often used words with more than one meaning to great effect. Also, you may wish to connect them with some of the historical events you will be studying."

"I would like that very much. I admit it was sometimes difficult for me to know exactly what Mr. Shakespeare was really saying."

"I'm afraid English literature, music and art are not my best fields. I prefer to read the older writers, all the way back to Aristotle, Plato and other distinguished greek and Roman gentlemen. When it comes to English writers, I rather like Geoffrey Chaucer, although his works are difficult to read since they are written in what we call Old English." Thomas asked if Harry liked poetry, and receiving an affirmative reply, went on, "You might find the poetry of Edmund Waller to your liking. I found the essays and poetry of Mr. Joseph Addison appealing. Unfortunately, he died a few years ago, in 1719, if I remember correctly. Everyone has, of course, read John Bunyan's *Pilgrim's Progress*. I daresay your education would be incomplete without that one. Then, of course, you will want to study art. No gentleman's education is complete without some knowledge of all the arts. You will want to study Rembrandt, Rubens, Titian, Jan Steen and many other master painters. I particularly enjoy the paintings of a Florentine painter named Andrea del Sarto. He was a bit before our time, the 15th and 16th century, I believe, but good painting is good painting whether new or old, don't you agree, Harry?"

"Yes, Sir, I do. I have not had the opportunity of visiting art galleries, but I look forward to doing so.

"If you are at all interested in philosophy, I recommend Thomas Hobbes, and since you expressed an interest in science, you will naturally want to read the works of our own Sir Isaac Newton who discovered gravity, and not so long ago at that, although I suppose it was always there." Thomas chuckled at his own joke and Harry also found it amusing. Thomas continued, "There was a Scottish physician who wrote several works on medicine, in case that interests you. His name was John Arbuthnot. For satire, there's none better than Samuel Butler. As for music, my favorite composer is Mr. Johann Sebastian Bach. And that, my boy, pretty much completes my list to recommend to you, however, I am sure the tutors I have in mind will have many more suggestions for you."

"Thank you, Uncle Thomas. I can hardly wait to begin my studies. I am even more eager to see the Great Thirkleby Hall, and also Mattersea, where my parents lived before moving to India."

"I think if we stop a time or two to rest, the horses can make it to Mattersea before dark, Harry. We can spend the night at your father's manor house. He keeps a retainer there, so it will be ready, and I notified the man that we would be coming sometime around this date. Since there is no cook there, we shall stop at the local tavern for dinner. Are you familiar with English cooking?"

"I really don't know, Uncle. I just ate whatever the cooks at home made for us. I know some of the dishes were definitely Indian, but I can only guess the others were English."

"Well, once you get to Thirsk, you will have plenty of our English fare. There are many who scoff at it and say it pales in comparison to that of France and other countries, but we who have eaten it all our lives, find it quite satisfying."

"I'm sure I'll enjoy it very much. May I ask a favor of you?"

"Of course, my boy, ask away."

"Please don't tell me when we are approaching our Mattersea home. My mother has described it so completely and so often that I believe I can recognize it from her description."

"Then by all means, we shall put you to the test. As for Great Thirkleby, I'd like to save it as a surprise as well. I am very proud of my home and will watch your expression as you get your first glimpse of it. We shall arrive there sometime tomorrow, and I expect Dinah will be at the door to greet you. Don't be surprised if she nearly knocks you over with her enthusiastic embrace. I expect Betty and young Dinah will be there as well. They may follow my wife's lead and embrace you heartily. On the other hand, they may be in one of their shyer moods and hang back from you. If that happens, please don't be offended. They'll be very friendly once they get to know you."

"It seems I have not yet outgrown the embraces of mothers and aunts and little sisters, but I have learned to endure them with good grace. I have not known my cousins, of course, but your daughters are probably very much like my sisters."

Thomas detected a drooping of Harry's eyes and suggested he take a bit of a nap before reaching Mattersea."

"I am tired and will try to follow your suggestion, but I am also enjoying the countryside scenery, it is so different from what I was used to in Bengal."

"Suit yourself, Harry, but remember the scenery will be here tomorrow and the days afterwards, or at least I hope it will be." With that, Harry leaned back in his seat inside the coach and promptly fell asleep.

Thomas woke him about a mile before they reached Mattersea so that Harry could test his ability to recognize the place from his mother's description.

"That one," he cried out when they rounded a bend in the road. "That's Mattersea. I know it."

"Right you are, my boy." The carriage stopped near the front door of the brick mansion, and Thomas directed Harry to bring his bags inside. He showed him the room his parents used when they lived there and suggested Harry might like to sleep in it that night. Once that was settled, the two returned to their carriage and headed for the local tavern where they enjoyed a hot kidney pie with rolls and a sweet.

Exploring the many rooms of Mattersea was a bittersweet experience for Harry. Imagining his parents' life there made him feel close in spirit to them but reminded him of how far apart they were in miles. Thinking of his brothers and sisters made his stomach hurt, and he found himself close to tears. When he regained control of his emotions, he joined his uncle in the huge library for a few minutes before retiring. Mattersea was beautiful, but he'd be glad to leave in the morning for Thirsk.

CHAPTER 8

▼

Harry felt refreshed after a good night's sleep in his parents' manor. The new day was cool and bright with a light wind blowing across open fields and through the trees, and Harry had regained his excitement over seeing Great Thirkleby Hall in Thirsk. Meanwhile, he was enjoying the English countryside as he and his uncle headed away from Mattersea. Uncle Thomas talked almost incessantly about Thirsk, Harry's education, English history, his own career in the navy, and anything else that popped into his mind. For most of the time, Harry listened with interest, but he was to a certain extent relieved when Thomas told him, "We are entering the town of Thirsk, now, Harry, and are at present crossing one of the two stone bridges over the River Colleck. We consider them to be rather elegant in design. Do you agree?"

"Yes, Uncle, I do. What are those ruins over to the left?"

"They were once a great castle which was built here by the Mowbray family in the year 979. It gives the town a rather melancholy cast, don't you think?"

"I agree, Uncle, but I suppose any ruin of a once great building would seem melancholy. That great church over yonder adds to that effect, too."

"It does, indeed, but it is a fine example of Gothic architecture."

"My brother Thomas will enjoy this sight when he comes." The jolt in his stomach at the mention of his brother's name convinced Harry that he'd be safer not mentioning his family or India for a while.

"It is not far now to Great Thirkleby Hall, Harry. Remember, I shall be watching for your reaction." Thomas smiled as he said this, letting Harry know he need not take him too seriously.

"I shall try to wear a pleasing expression, Uncle Thomas." He received a fond pat on the head for his reply.

As the coach turned into a long driveway lined with Scotch fir, Harry could see that it was not straight, but curved to conform to the land. Soon he caught his first glimpse of a quaint Jacobean house situated atop a small rise on the northwest side of the village. It was set within a spacious wooded park. Uncle Thomas pointed out cedars of Lebanon, Wellingtonia Gigantia, and purple beeches. Close to the house he saw a neat lawn surrounded by shrubbery and clumps of bright flowers.

"Oh, Uncle Thomas, it's a castle," Harry observed with no need to put on a false expression of awe. "I've never seen a house like it. What is it called?"

"It's Jacobean. It is a form of architecture popular about 100 years ago and combines elements of German, Flemish and Elizabethan styles. As you can see, it is built of brick with stone dressings. Notice the capped turrets and the Flemish gables. It has three floors and eight fire rooms. You can't see all eight chimneys from here, but I assure you they do exist." The horses came to a stop outside the huge oak front door with stained glass panels on either side. "Come along, we'll go inside and meet your Aunt Dinah."

Harry was quite taken by the large entry room, its high ceiling and its Wainscoted walls which shone from a coating of oil. He would be given a tour of the house later, but now his Aunt Dinah made her appearance, and as predicted by Thomas, put out her arms to Harry to give him a motherly embrace. "I'm so glad you arrived safely, Harry. Welcome to Thirkleby. We are so happy to have you stay with us."

"Thank you, Aunt, I am glad to be here. Your home is very beautiful."

"Thank you, Harry. You must be tired from all your travels. I'll show you to your room, and you can rest a bit before supper." She led him to a large, square room on the second floor. Its walls were plastered and painted in blue. On the side wall hung a suit of Imagery Tapestry hangings, showing scenes of fox hunts and riders wearing red jackets. The bed was a four-posted one with a white calico canopy. A blue and white quilted counterpane was lain over the feather-filled mattress. In one corner was a small stand with a wash basin and bowl, along with a blue towel. There were two high chests of drawers and two banister-back chairs in the room, and Harry was pleased to see there was a corner where he could put his bookcase from the ship and his books. He thought his writing desk would also fit in. He would be very comfortable here. He walked over to the window and looked out over the Hambleton Hills on one side and the churches of Topcliffe and Baldersby on the other.

As the family gathered for the evening meal, Sir Thomas more formally welcomed Harry to Thirkleby. He quoted a few lines of poetry. "Welcome to Great Thirkleby, Harry—'*Where comes no guest, but is allow'd to eate Without his feare, and of the Lord's owne meate; Where the same beere, and bread, and self-same wine, That is his Lordship's, shall be also mine.*' Perhaps I should change that last word to 'thine', eh, Harry?"

Dinah shook her head and spoke, "Oh, Thomas, you and your poetry. You know the boy is far too young for beer and wine."

Thomas rolled his eyes at Harry, "My beloved wife sometimes takes things much too literally. Pay her no mind." He leaned toward Dinah and gave her a brief kiss on her cheek. It was Dinah's turn to roll her eyes.

The main course at supper that evening consisted of roasted fowl. All present stood while Thomas asked a blessing. They ate from pewter plates with the new two-tined forks that had recently come into vogue. Afterwards, Thomas invited Harry to join him in the parlor where stood a table with six joined stools, several cane-back chairs and a chest on which were displayed pieces of silver, four trencher plates and Aunt Dinah's collection of silver salt cellars. "I shan't keep you long, Harry, but I want to go over our routine with you. You will no doubt awaken in the morning when you hear the breakfast bell ring. You need not hurry. It is rung early to give you time to wash up and get dressed. When we are all gathered around the table, the serving girl will bring in our food. I think you will find a good display to choose from. After breakfast you and I should go around to see the history tutor I told you about. I think that's a good starting place for your studies. Do you agree?"

"I do, and while there is much history I want to know about, I think Yorkshire itself should be first. After all, I'll be living here for quite some time. I should know as much as possible about it.

The tutor lived in the center of town in lodgings provided by the pharmacist's wife in their home. His name was Peter Partridge, and though he appeared but a little older than Harry, he was, in fact, twenty-two and well educated. He was a thin and rather pale young man, but he had a friendly smile which showed a wide space between his two front teeth. The most careful combing could not make his hair lay flat over his protruding ears.

"So, Master Harry, you're ready to learn a bit about our fair Riding!" he remarked. "A splendid starting point and one with which I am completely familiar, having been born here and lived here all my life. You can be sure your lessons will not always keep you indoors, for it will be my great pleasure to show you places of interest within walking distance."

Uncle Thomas spoke up. "You may borrow my coach and horses if you would like to go farther afield, Master Peter. I want my nephew to get a good grounding in local history."

"That's very generous of you, Sir Frankland. Master Harry is a fortunate lad and I a fortunate tutor. Shall we start our lessons tomorrow?"

The hour was set and the Franklands returned to Thirkleby where Sir Thomas had work to do in connection with his position as Lord of the Admiralty. This position, which prior to the 15th century had consisted of three individual courts, had by now been merged into one High Admiralty Court, presided over by one Admiral. The court had a marshal and various other officers and forms of legal process, and its jurisdiction covered all crimes and offenses involving English ships or crews that were committed at sea or along the English coast outside the borders of any county. This jurisdiction was formally conferred on the Lord High Admiralty in the 16th century. About that time the Admiralty Court acquired jurisdiction over commercial and other cases properly belonging to the common-law courts. The maritime wars of the 18th century gave widened scope to the exercise of its prize jurisdiction, the distribution of the cargo captured during these wars. The Admiralty's headquarters were in Portsmouth, but Sir Thomas was able to do much of his work at home.

Peter Partridge arrived at Great Thirkleby Hall precisely on the hour decided upon and promptly began to give Harry his first lesson on York history. "Master Harry, did you know the Romans first came to Britain in the year 55 B.C.?"

"No, I was not aware of that. What brought them here?"

"They came on a raiding party, led by none other than Julius Caesar himself. He must have thought it would be an easy victory, but he was wrong. They returned in A.D. 43 with the intention of conquering the Brigantes. This was a group, you might call them a tribe, of people living in the mountainous area of England. In the historian Ptolemy's book of geography written in 140 A.D., York was listed as one of nine places in the territory held by the Brigantes. It was thought to include the North and West Ridings of Yorkshire as well. Those Brigantes were a feisty bunch with much rivalry between noble families and the chiefs. This made it very difficult to control them, so there were many power struggles among them. In 71 A.D. the Romans established a military base of their 9th Legion to fight against those pesky Brigantes. The base remained the headquarters of the Roman army in North Britain for over 300 years. The Brigantes actually lived outside the Roman area and the Romans kept them pretty much under control by means of an alliance with their queen Cartimandua and by pouring a great deal of money into that effort. According to the Roman historian Tacitus, they had to help out Queen Cartimandua at least three different times. And guess who her main rival was—her own husband, a fellow by the name of Venutius. He was a powerful and ambitious man and not always trustworthy. Tacitus hinted that Queen Cartimandua was not exactly what you call a faithful wife, and that was what caused the trouble with her husband, but my studies have led me to the conclusion that the struggles of those times were politically motivated. Anyway, Venutius took advantage of civil strife in the empire in 69-70 and the fact that British legions were divided in their loyalties, and he seized power and exiled Queen Cartimandua."

Harry was totally fascinated by all that Peter told him and eagerly awaited whatever information would come next. Peter continued, "The Romans' military base here in York, which, by the way, was called Eburacom in those days, which meant "The place where yew trees grow", was their most important one, even greater than their other two permanent fortresses in Chester and Caerlon. It was so important that several Roman emperors visited here, and two of them, Septimus Severus, who governed the Roman Empire from 208 to 211, and Constantius I, who was called Chlorus, died here—Severus in A.D. 211, and Constantius in A.D. 306. Constantius was the father of Constantine the Great. I'll tell you more of his exploits later on. When we visit York you will see remnants of the Roman fortress and Hadrian's Wall, which was built from 122 to 138. The original fortress was rebuilt in stone around 100, rebuilt again in the 200's, and around 300 was partially rebuilt in a much grander style. By the third and fourth centuries A.D. York had been made the capital of Lower Britain. Can you guess what the other capital was?"

"London?"

"Good show, Master Harry. Dead on. In those centuries we believe there was much more here than just the army of Rome. Commerce thrived, and there were palaces and luxurious homes. We think it was possible to have a happy family life here in those days especially if you were wealthy. On the other hand, there were also poor homes and humble workshops, to say nothing of slaves. The one good thing was that it was possible for a slave to actually become his master's heir. Amazing, don't you agree?"

Harry could barely comprehend that all this took place more than one thousand years ago. He replied to Peter's question, "I should never have suspected that, Peter, but I should like to know more about that wall you mentioned. Who was Hadrian? Why did he build the wall? How long was it? Can we see it some day?"

"Slow down, Harry. Those are all good questions and I am very much pleased that you are so interested. Let me answer your questions one at a time. Hadrian was the Emperor of the Roman Empire beginning in the year 117. At that time the Empire took in practically all the known world, that is, most of what is now Europe and some of Africa, particularly the northernmost parts. With the invasion of Britain, it was extended to its fullest extent. Hadrian realized this. He knew it would be impractical for many reasons to capture more land. We believe he built the wall as a boundary line of the Roman Empire. Some think it was for protection from various tribes, but I agree with those who say it was a boundary because the Romans were quite capable of handling any troublesome tribes in the area. In short, they didn't need that protection. Having said this, I must tell you that the wall was eighty Roman miles long, which is about seventy-four miles by our standards today. Most of it was made of stone, which was readily available in the area. Where stone was not about, those sections were made of wood and turf. All along the wall were mileposts and forts, so that does give some weight to the protection argument, doesn't it?"

"I would like to know which theory is the correct one, Peter."

"So would I, Harry. At any rate, you asked about Hadrian himself. He was born in Spain." Harry looked very surprised to learn that. Peter continued, "I forgot to tell you that many of the soldiers and even the leaders of the Roman Empire were not born in Rome but came from many other places, particularly places the Romans had previously conquered. Hadrian was a noted architect. It was he who designed the Pantheon in Rome. The wall was really quite an architectural accomplishment. It was ten feet thick in places and encompassed three fortified bridges over the rivers. It followed the lay of the land in most cases, going up over hills and down in the lower lands. Perhaps we can read more about Hadrian one of these days." Peter smiled broadly at Harry. "I cannot tell you how pleased I am that you exhibit so much interest in this subject. As I mentioned, the Romans invaded and captured many lands, but it was not as bad as you might think for the captured people. The Romans brought with them their own ways, which included laws, something many of the tribes had not had. The forts along the wall brought business to those areas and many small towns grew up outside the forts. For many, life with the Romans was far better than it had been without them."

"I doubt it would be like that if we were captured by some foreign army today, Peter."

"I agree, but these are different times. Let us continue. The people were thriving, towns were growing, everything seemed to be going quite smoothly. Then came disaster. In about 450 there was a terrible flood in the area which destroyed the lower parts of the town and the bridge over the River Ouse."

Harry listened intently as Peter spoke on for the remainder of the hour, imparting an extensive knowledge of the various campaigns of the Roman Legions across various parts of Britain. He ended by repeating that he hoped Master Harry would get to see York soon, especially the magnificent cathedral there at the Minster, which was built diagonally across the exact spot where the Roman fortress once stood.

Harry knew he was going to enjoy his lessons with Peter Partridge and hoped the young tutor would be around for a long time.

Within a few days Harry was introduced to his other three tutors. Mr. Geoffrey Broadbent would teach him all about English literature from Chaucer to the present. They agreed to start with Harry's favorite, William Shakespeare. Geoffrey was delighted to learn that Harry had already read several of the Bard's more popular plays. Harry was delighted with Geoffrey's keen insight into the minds of the characters and his background in the history involved. Broadbent aspired to a career on stage and was doing tutelage until he could succeed in that endeavor. He had a loud and stentorian voice, and Lady Frankland, plying her needle two rooms away, was startled to hear on occasion such well-known lines as "A horse, a horse, my kingdom for a horse" and "Once more unto the breach, dear friends, once more" emanating from the classroom. When the would-be actor bellowed out a line from "King Lear" at top voice: "Thou'lt come no more, never, never, never, never, never." Lady Frankland smiled and thought, "I hope not. If the 'nevers' get any louder, I'll have to remove myself to a far corner of the house."

Harry preferred to hear Geoffrey's reading of all the parts, but he was once in a while goaded into reading one himself. He outright refused to read Juliet and had to try mightily not to laugh when Geoffrey pitched his voice up an octave or more to cry out, "Romeo, Romeo, wherefore art thou Romeo?"

For his instruction in the arts, Sir Thomas had selected Lawrence Ashbury. A very large man, Ashbury also revealed a pomposity and condescension that proved irritating to Harry. His very first words were, "Tell me all you know about Rembrandt Van Rijn, young man."

Harry replied that he had not made the gentleman's acquaintance but had heard the name from his uncle. "Was he an artist? Or was he an author, or a poet?" he asked.

"An author or a poet? Unbelievable! I certainly have my work cut out for me, don't I?" Similar remarks were forthcoming regularly, and Harry did not look forward to his sessions with this unpleasant man. He thought to himself, I came here to be educated. If I were already educated, I needn't have come at all. However, rather than risk embarrassing his uncle, he kept these thoughts to himself.

The last of his tutors was an elderly man who had taught science at a boys school for many years and was now retired except for an occasional stint of tutoring. While pleasant enough, he tended to drone on and on, and Harry found it difficult to stay awake during his discourse, let alone concentrate on the material being presented.

When he had been attending to these studies for about a month, Sir Thomas called him to his study for an evaluation of his tutors. Harry told his uncle how much he enjoyed his sessions with Peter and Geoffrey. "They make learning so enjoyable, Uncle Thomas. You should hear Geoffrey when he reads Mr. Shakespeare's lines. He puts his whole heart into it. I think he will one day succeed in his desire to perform on stage." He went on to describe the negative aspects of the other tutors.

"My boy, you should have brought these to my attention immediately. You should not be made to bear these boring and demeaning sessions. I shall dismiss them both. There are plenty of good tutors around. We'll find ones that are more acceptable." Harry expressed his relief and gratitude and looked forward to meeting two new instructors.

Sir Thomas spoke, "I have another subject to discuss with you, Harry. You have been here well over a month now and have not yet asked for any money."

"I have not needed any, Sir. Aunt Dinah has given me enough to provide Peter and myself with a meal or a treat when we have gone on some of our walking tours."

"Is there nothing you would like? You know your father sent me a generous sum for your use."

"I have noticed that my shirts fall short of my wrists these days, and my shoes begin to pinch if I walk very far in them. I must have grown since I left Bengal."

"There you go. We shall have a splendid shopping trip soon and outfit you in all the things a young lad of your standing should have, which surely will include a warm coat for the coming winter, which I assure you will be much colder than what you have been used to in Bengal."

CHAPTER 9

▼

Harry had been at Thirsk going on two years now. They had been productive years, and he had grown, not only in stature, but in knowledge and culture. Always a polite boy, he now possessed the polished manners of an aristocratic young man. He was well grounded in the history of Britain and the outside world. He had read voraciously, studied all the science he could find, and developed what would be a life-long passion for botany and landscape-gardening. Presently he was involved in redesigning the gardens at Great Thirkleby Hall, with the permission of Sir Thomas, who admitted to having neglected that area for some time. Best of all, he had just received the good news that his younger brother Thomas was due to arrive in England in a few more days. Sir Thomas inquired after the location of the ship Thomas was on, and just yesterday heard from the captain of a Dutch merchant vessel that it was already in the Bay of Biscay. He estimated that it would arrive at Gravesend on Friday.

Since Sir Thomas had business in London on Thursday, it was decided that Harry would accompany him, and they would stay there until Thomas's ship arrived in port. "After all, there are still many things for you to do and see in our greatest city," his uncle told him. "If Thomas's ship is delayed, we'll go sightseeing. If he comes on time, the three of us can go to a few places before returning to Thirsk."

Harry was unusually keyed up at the thought of seeing his brother, and he especially looked forward to sharing his tutors with him. Uncle Thomas had decreed that once Thomas arrived, both boys should study French, Latin, and mathematics, and learn to ride horses and to dance. The horses were of enormous interest to Harry. He had seen the excitement of fox hunts hosted by some of Sir

Thomas's friends and wanted desperately to take part in one. He wanted to wear a red coat and ride like the wind on a fleet-footed horse. He wanted the excitement of being first to catch up with the fox. Just hearing the sound of the horn that set the race in motion was enough to excite him. The dancing was of little interest to him, but he supposed that a young man of his social rank would be obliged to learn that, too. Hopefully, the minuet would not be included in his lessons. He had watched his parents dance that dance with their friends and could not imagine himself bowing and scraping as they had.

Standing at the dock with the crowds awaiting arriving passengers, Harry was the first to spot Thomas's ship. As it pulled into the pier, he saw his brother hanging so far over the ship's rail in an effort to find him that Harry feared he'd fall into the water. Harry shouted and waved, at last getting his brother's attention. Thomas ran off the ramp with arms open for a big brotherly embrace. He was filled with excitement, and Sir Thomas had all he could do to get him to concentrate on the business of his furniture, deciding in the end that they would sell it. They found one of the men in the business of buying and selling such goods and with some expert negotiating by Sir Thomas, received a satisfactory price.

After inquiring after the other members of his family and hearing that all were well, Harry asked Thomas about his journey from Bengal and learned the reason for his brother's extreme enthusiasm. "It was wonderful, Harry. I loved every minute of it. It's what I want to do. I want to join His Majesty's navy when I turn eighteen."

Sir Thomas, sensing that this was more than just a young boy's infatuation with the sea, told his nephew, "With your enthusiasm and my contacts, you could expect a fine career in the navy."

"I would like one day to be Captain of my own ship," the younger Thomas told him.

"Why not aim for Admiral, Thomas? I did it, and you can as well. What was it that formed this idea in your mind, if you don't object to my asking?"

"Not at all, Sir. We ran afoul of a pirate ship off the shore of Portugal, and I was awed by the masterful maneuvering of our ship by the captain. It was wonderful to see him heel and turn, dodging the pirate at every turn, and finally outrunning him. I decided then and there that was what I wanted to spend my adult life doing."

"It is not for everyone, but for those who love the sea and ships, it can be most satisfying. I believe you may be one of those people."

It was dark the next evening when they reached Thirsk. Sir Thomas suggested they all retire early so that they might get a good start on showing Thomas the house and grounds the next day. He thought they could postpone lessons for a few days while he became acquainted with the area and had free time to enjoy his reunion with Harry.

The riding instructor for the boys was the groomsman at one of the neighboring estates. Sir Thomas outfitted the boys in jodhpurs and boots, handsome jackets and the traditional plush derby. Neither boy had the slightest fear of the big animals and quickly mastered the basics of riding. Soon they were galloping across the open fields, exhilarated by the wind in their faces, the grace and speed of the animals, and the feeling of being in command of the horses and their lives, at least at that moment.

Dancing lessons, were quite a different thing. Their instructor was a somewhat effeminate older man, small in stature and possessing what the boys called a prissy manner of speaking. "Now, gentlemen," he announced, "we will start with the minuet." The boys groaned simultaneously. All that balancing, bowing and toe pointing was just too foppish for their taste. They groaned more when their dance master informed them that they would be taking turns learning the gentleman's steps and the lady's.

"You mean you want us to dance together?" Harry inquired unbelievingly.

"Do you see any young ladies present, Master Harry? I do not. Of course, you must dance together or I shall have to be partner to each of you in turn."

The brothers looked at each other and quickly decided dancing together was preferable to that alternative.

In this way were the lives of the two young Franklands ordered for the next several years. Much study was relieved by riding their horses around the countryside and by many trips with Sir Thomas to visit the places throughout England that Sir Henry had once described to them. Soon it was time for Harry's eighteenth birthday, a milestone in the life of any young man and particularly one of aristocratic breeding. Sir Thomas generously offered to organize a foxhunt to celebrate the occasion, the first in which Harry would actively participate.

May 10, 1734, turned out to be a perfect day for the hunt with bright sunshine and cool breezes. It was to be an all-gentlemen day. The men would join the young ladies that evening for the dance to be held in the ballroom of Great Thirkleby Hall. Aunt Dinah, with help from her daughters and the serving girl, had decorated the room with streamers and candles in sconces along the walls. An orchestra of five musicians had been hired for the occasion.

The sons of Sir Thomas's neighbors, friends, and colleagues arrived on horseback for the fox hunt, resplendent in their colorful jackets and wielding their crops in imitation of the jousting sticks of olden days. When all had arrived, Sir Thomas raised his stirrup cup in a toast to his nephew, wishing him years of happiness and many more birthdays. Harry delighted in the sounds of the hunt, the yapping dogs eager to get started, the clink of the cups, the noisy chatter among the riders, the snorting of the horses. When Sir Thomas raised his ivory-handled pistol into the air and fired one shot, the caged fox was released and began the run for his life. When he had been given a fair chance to get away, the dogs were let loose, Sir Thomas blew his horn and cried out, "Tally Ho," and the chase was on. The riders followed wherever the fox and the hounds led them, across fields, through wooded areas, swamps, and brush. Excitement was in the air. No one really cared about the fox or his fate if he were caught by the hounds; it was just good, out-door, male exuberance that the riders were caught up in. This particular fox was slyer than most, and the hunt continued for several hours before he was at last pinned down. Laughing and shouting, the riders returned to the Hall where they were served a hearty feast of roast fowl, pork, beans, vegetables, and such delightful desserts as fruit pies and rich cakes, and all the wine they cared to imbibe.

That evening a number of young ladies arrived in resplendent attire for the dance. Their fathers joined Sir Thomas in the library to smoke cigars, drink whiskey, and discuss the political affairs of the day. The girls' mothers sat around the perimeter of the ballroom to keep an eye on the proceedings and make sure nothing improper occurred. At last the torture of learning all the current dance steps was about to pay off for Harry Frankland. Besides having his brother Thomas as a partner, his Aunt Dinah had occasionally volunteered her services to give him at least some practice with a female. On occasion his cousins Betty and Dinah served as his partners. He was quite confident that he could perform the steps accurately and with some grace, and he had already observed that several of the young ladies present were eyeing him with interest. Little wonder! He had grown to be a fine-looking young man, taller than many of his peers and well built. The young ladies were exclaiming to their mothers that they thought his features were quite noble and refined. They felt he had a somewhat pensive, almost melancholy, expression, although nothing in his life with the possible exception of being isolated from his parents and younger siblings would account for that. His black hair was thick and neatly combed, and his long-lashed blue eyes sent shivers through many a young maiden. Surprisingly, the mothers reacted in much the same way as their daughters, greeting him with simpering smiles as he passed; the bolder ones reaching out to touch his hand in greeting.

He told Thomas afterwards that it had been a very pleasant evening and that he looked forward to attending future dances and balls. He would not have to wait long. The invitations began arriving within the week. He was equally popular with the other young men, who quickly recognized that he had been well educated, was above average in intelligence, and possessed not only a discerning nature which allowed him to get quickly to the heart of any matter and express a thoughtful opinion thereon, but also a quick wit, a quality much admired by the aristocracy at that time.

Noting that his nephew was so well received, Sir Thomas began discreetly to introduce Harry to some of his own peers and colleagues. Soon Harry counted among his friends Mr. Horace Walpole, who was just one year younger than himself. Walpole, whose given name was Horatio, was the 4th Earl of Oxford and the son of Sir Robert Walpole, Prime Minister. The younger Walpole had a reputation as a writer, as well as being a noted connoisseur and collector of art. He would eventually enter Parliament.[1]

Another friend was Henry Fielding, the novelist, who was Harry's senior by some eleven years. After graduating from Eton, Fielding was quoted as saying, "Having no choice but to be a hackney-writer or a hackney-coachman, I chose the former." Fielding had enjoyed a successful career in writing for theater, beginning in 1725 with "Love in Several Masques" and followed in 1730 by "The Author's Farce" and "Rape Upon Rape; or, the Justice Caught in His Own Trap". It was also in 1730 that he wrote his most remembered play, a burlesque titled "Tom Thumb, A Tragedy". Unfortunately, in 1737 his sarcasm went too far. His "Pasquin" and "Historical Register, for the Year 1736" at the Little Theatre in the Hay were merciless in ridiculing Sir Robert Walpole, who, in retaliation, pushed through Parliament the Licensing Act by which all new plays had to be approved and licensed by the Lord Chamberlain before production. Fielding would thereafter write no more plays.[2] He turned to writing novels.

Sir Philip Dormer Stanhope, 4th Earl of Chesterfield, whose looks and manners were so similar to Harry's own that the two were sometimes mistaken for uncle and nephew, was another of his companions. Lord Chesterfield was a statesman, diplomat and noted wit. He also opposed Sir Robert Walpole and served as Ambassador to Holland in 1728[3].

One evening in 1738 Sir Thomas asked Harry to accompany him to his study. Harry, of course, obliged him, wondering what was on his uncle's mind. "I have just received some sad news, Nephew," the older man began. "It seems my brother Henry, your father, has passed away. There were few details in the message I received, so I cannot give you more information. Perhaps we shall learn more later, but for now, we can only mourn his passing. He is a great loss to both of us."

Harry, having never considered the possibility of losing a parent, felt a great jumble of feelings wash over him. Sadness was paramount, but was it sadness because he would never see his dear parent again or sadness because he had seen so little of him during his lifetime? He had known that his father loved him, but Sir Henry was so occupied with his duties as Governor of the Bengal factory, that he had little time for his large family. It had been several years since father and son had been together and then only for brief visits when the elder Frankland was in England on business for the East India Company.

He went to his uncle and clasped him on the shoulder. "This is a sad time for both of us, Uncle. I shall miss knowing he is in Bengal. In truth, Uncle, you have beenmore like a father to me these last years. I hope you realize how grateful I am to you for every effort you have made in my behalf."

"Thank you, Son. Your Aunt Dinah and I have counted ourselves fortunate to have had you, and later your brother Thomas, living in our home."

"Was there any word of my mother's plans, Uncle?"

"Yes. I should have told you straight away. She and your siblings will in time return to Mattersea to live. I'm sure you will be glad to see them."

Although Harry did not at that moment give a thought to the subject, he was now, at age 22, in possession of an ample fortune and would soon hold some influence at the court of King George II. Never had he considered the honor which would come his way in the next three years. He learned eventually of the death in America of one Jonathan Belcher, followed by that of John Jekyl, which left the position of Collector of the Port of Boston vacant. At the same time it became necessary to fill the post of Governor of Massachusetts. By then Harry's popularity prompted the Duke of Newcastle, at the time secretary of the southern department of colonial affairs, to offer the choice of those two offices to him.

Harry's only competition for the post of his choice was Sir William Shirley who had already lived in Boston for seven years. The office of collector being more lucrative, both Shirley and his lovely and talented Lady Frances, who happened to be in London at the time, made a strong bid for that post. Perhaps in deference to Sir Thomas or perhaps for other reasons, the decision was at last made to give the governorship to Mr. Shirley and the collectorship to Harry Frankland. Harry was now one step closer to meeting the young woman who would have such a profound effect on his life.

Notes: 1. Horace (born Horatio) Walpole, 4th Earl of Oxford, 1717-1797. Author of the horror tale, "The Castle of Otranto" in 1765, which was to begin the vogue for Gothic romances. He was a prolific letter writer as well as author of both fiction and nonfiction. His tragedy, "The Mysterious Mother" was published in 1768, "Historic Doubts on the Life and Reign of King Richard, the 3rd" in 1768, and "Anecdotes of Painting in England" in four volumes from 1762-1771.

2. Henry Fielding, born April 22, 1707 and died October 8, 1754 (in Lisbon, Portugal). Author of "Pamela; or Virtue Rewarded", considered to be the first English novel. This was the story of a young serving girl who so steadfastly refused her master's efforts to seduce her that he married her. This was read by many English women, who called out for more books of that type. Most books of that era were about goodness overcoming evil, morality or lack thereof, etc. From 1739 to 1741 Fielding wrote and edited a three-times-a-week newspaper, "The Champion; or, British Mercury". His book "Joseph Andrews" came out in 1742, and his best known, "Tom Jones" in 1749.

3. Lord Chesterfield wrote: "Letters to His Son" and "Letters to his Godson", considered by some to be excellent guides to good manners, the art of pleasing, and the art of worldly success. While many found the "Letters" to be charming and witty, Samuel Johnson described them as teaching "the morals of a whore, and the manners of a dancing master", primarily because they concentrated too much for his taste on the subject of obtaining worldly ends.

CHAPTER 10

▼

Sir Thomas knocked lightly on the door to Harry's bedroom. "May I come in?" he called.

"Of course, Uncle. You are always welcome."

"Are you nearly packed?"

"Just a few more items, and I'll be ready to go." Harry assured him.

"You realize, Harry, that you are following somewhat in the footsteps of one of my favorite poets as you embark on your new career."

"What do you mean, Uncle?" Harry inquired.

"I speak of Chaucer. He was not only a great poet, but he was at one time the Comptroller of the Customs in the Port of London. Did you get to read any of his poems?"

"I'm afraid not, Uncle. Did I miss out on a good thing?" Harry asked.

"Ah, Harry, you must some day read "A Nun's Priest's Tale." Thomas had a broad grin on his face as he said this. "If you'll wait a moment, I'll get my copy and read a bit of it to you."

Harry heard his uncle chuckling as he headed toward the library. He continued his packing, wondering what the older man was up to.

Thomas returned quickly. "Put my hand right to it, Harry," he announced well pleased with himself. "Now listen to this: "A Povre widwe, somdel stope in age, Was whylom dwelling in a narwe cotage. Bisyde a grove; stonding in a dale. This widwe, of which I telle yow my tale, Sin thilke day that she was last a wyf."

"Enough, Uncle," Harry interrupted. "I don't speak or understand whatever language you are prattling in."

"Why, Nephew, it's English. I can't believe you're not enthralled. You may be astonished to learn that when I was about your present age, I hired a tutor to teach me to read Chaucer aloud and to interpret it for me. I admit it took weeks of practice before I could do it correctly. Even now I reread some of his works fairly regularly in order not to lose my ability to do so. In spite of your initial reaction, I think you might still get some satisfaction from reading some of his writing. In the poem I read from, our Geoffrey wrote on in that vein for about a dozen or more pages. There was a most memorable Chauntecleer, a fox named Russel, cows, calves, dogs. I'm sure it would remind you of our many fox hunts."

"Thank you, but I do believe I will remember our foxhunts without help from Mr. Chaucer."

"You know, Harry, I have always regretted not having studied the evolution of the English language. Do you not also wonder how it changed from Chaucer's day to ours? Do you think it will change more in the future? What about the colonists in America that you will soon be joining, do you think they will develop their own expressions and idioms, their own speech patterns, in time? I suppose they may, but I would hope not so much change that communication between our countrymen becomes difficult."

Harry closed his trunk and looked thoughtfully at his uncle, the man who had been more like a father to him than his own parent. "Uncle Thomas, I have had much good fortune in my life, and I do not mean to complain, but it seems whenever the best things come my way, they come with a price, and it's always the same price. Will it always be this way?"

"I assume you mean leaving your family. Am I correct?"

"Yes. Coming here was the best thing that could have happened to me, but it meant leaving my parents and my brothers and sisters behind. Do you know how difficult that was for a twelve-year-old boy?" Thomas said nothing but nodded his head to show he understood.

"Now I have been given an opportunity rarely given to men of my age. Being Collector at the Port of Boston will doubtless allow me to play an influential part in the life of that entire colony, or certainly in that part which has to do with commerce and shipping. Who can guess what may yet come to me as a result of this appointment? There may be no limit to how far I can go, but, once again, the price is leaving all the people I love most in the world. My dear mother has been in England little more than two years now. We were separated by nearly ten years, yet when we came together again, it was almost as if we had never been apart. There are strong ties that bind my mother and myself together, whether we are near or far from each other, and I am grateful that it is so. Now I must leave her again, not knowing if we shall ever see each other in the years ahead. My brother Thomas has already joined the navy, and we see little of each other. Surely, we will see less when I am in the colonies and he is off to the seven seas. And Annie, my precious Annie. She is already becoming a young lady, and we can expect she will be a wife in the not too distant future. I know not where she will be or if I will ever again see her sweet face."

Sir Thomas was nearly at a loss for words. He could feel the depth of his nephew's grief, but could do nothing to assuage it.

Harry went on, "While the negotiations were going on as to whether William Shirley or I would be the Collector, my only thoughts were of winning the position. I was gratified beyond words when the choice was made known. I could foresee nothing but a brilliant future for myself wherein I would be doing useful work and making a contribution of some value to my king, my country, and the colonies. Where have those thoughts gone? Why can I now think not of what I have to gain, but only of what I am about to lose?"

"My Boy, we all feel that way when we leave those we love, but you must never think of it as loss. You will never lose your mother's sweet love, nor your sister's. You will always be their respected and adored eldest brother to your other siblings. I have no wish to embarrass you, Harry, but I must add that you will never be without the love of your Aunt Dinah and myself. You and Thomas filled the void in our family since we had no sons of our own. Now, go on to whatever great adventures await you, and know there is every chance that fate will once again bring you into the company of some, if not all, of us."

"Dear Uncle, I thank you from the bottom of my heart for your words. Just as my father's words to me before I left Bengal helped me to focus on the future, you have renewed my enthusiasm for my career. I shall, of course, visit Mother on my way to London and the ship that will carry me to the colonies. I trust I will control myself such that we part on a happy note. Now I'll say good-bye to Aunt Dinah, and we can be on our way, and," he stopped to grin at his beloved uncle, "I shall do all in my power to preserve the English language as it is today."

The voyage across the Atlantic Ocean to Massachusetts was of much shorter duration than the long voyage ten years ago from Bengal. The ship that carried Harry Frankland to the Massachusetts Bay colony arrived at Boston Harbor in two months' time. Although he had promised to write his mother on his arrival, he chose to get acquainted with his new home and begin his new work before doing so. There would be much more to say by waiting. When at last he had settled into his new quarters and learned what duties his new position would entail, he took pen in hand and began what would be a lengthy letter.

My dearest Mother,

I arrived safely in Boston Harbor not quite a fortnight ago. I have found a very comfortable house to live in. It does not compare to Great Thirkleby Hall but is more than adequate for my needs at present. I have also employed a staff to run my household, so I am well settled in.

Mother, I hardly know where to begin. I have met William Shirley, and despite our each seeking the same position, I believe we can become congenial acquaintances if not dear friends. I find we have much in common. He is a well-born gentleman as well as a highly educated one. We share a common love of England, and, being Episcopalians, we worship side by side at the King's Chapel. I believe the Duke of Newcastle and his advisors made the correct decision, as Mr. Shirley is eminently well suited to governing the colony, and my talents may be put to better use as collector. We shall soon find out if I am correct in this.

You may find this an amusing story. It seems on the evening of the day when The Massachusetts Bay citizens received the news that the Royal Commission had appointed William Shirley as Governor, they put on a fine fireworks show from the top of the Town House. One of the Serpents fell into the Town House Lanthorn where all the remaining fireworks were stored and set them all off at once. They tell me it was a particularly pretty sight, but some men in the Lanthorn were scorched (not too seriously, Praise Be) and a few windows were broken. This was written up in the Boston Gazette on August 10, and people are still talking about it. (NOTE: A lanthorn is a square, circular, elliptical or polygonal erection on the top of a dome, having pierced sides fitted with windows to let in light. A Serpent is a type of fireworks which burns with a serpentine motion of flame. The above probably refers to "Squibbs Serpentes Rockettes".)

Dear Mother, I have the highest admiration for the settlers of the Massachusetts Bay Colony. Can you imagine what it was like for those people? They traveled for months aboard a small vessel, not knowing what to expect when they arrived here. They first stepped on this continent's soil at Plymouth a mere 120 years ago. There were no inns where they could find a warm bath, hot food, and a bed for the night. All they had was what they had brought with them. Their homes, their defenses, everything they needed had to be made from materials at hand. I understand many died of starvation that first cold winter. Fortunately, they managed a good relationship with the natives, at least for a while. Now, in the city of Boston alone there are 16,000 inhabitants, with about 1500 of them being slaves of African origin. I have learned that this year alone there have been some 40 sailing vessels on the stocks, and they tell me it has the most commerce of any of the English colonies in America. Over 600 ships have gone out from here, laden with freight, and headed for foreign ports.

I sometimes think I have never left London. I quickly became quite comfortable here. There are ten churches here and the Town House mentioned above is most impressive. A prosperous merchant, Mr. Peter Faneuil, Esq. is at this very time in the process of building a large market and hall to be given to the use of the public. And the people! They are as English as you or I, particularly those of wealth and aristocratic backgrounds. Everything about them speaks of our beloved England, their speech, their dress, their homes, furniture—everything. They do their utmost to keep up with the fads and fashions of London. Every passenger arriving from England is quickly besieged with questions as to what is going on back there. All the major offices here are filled with influential men from England, and they lead society and establish its customs. Whenever a problem of society or politics or government arises, the question is asked, "What would they have done at court?"

The most wealthy gentlemen and their ladies tend to own estates and manor houses in the north end of town. Perhaps one day I, too, will live there.

I was pleasantly surprised to learn that there are at present a wide variety of newspapers here. I believe the oldest is the "Boston News-Letter", which began back in 1704. Then came the "Boston Gazette", the "Boston Weekly Post-Boy", the "Boston Evening Post" and a brand new one just this year, the "New England Weekly Journal"

You may remember my good friend Henry Fielding. Just this day I learned that his novel "Pamela" has reached our shores, and the ladies of Boston are eagerly reading it and comparing their opinions of it whenever they gather together. They are all hoping he will write another novel soon, and I am sure that hope will be realized. I must write and congratulate Henry on his success in his chosen field.

I believe Uncle Thomas would enjoy it here, since anyone bearing the title of Baronet is treated with the utmost respect and deference. Simply travelling in a coach and four with armorial bearing and servants resplendent in livery is enough to protect the owner from any possible indignities. It appears the lesser folk here look upon any piece of paper stamped with the crown as being something almost sacred. Thomas might well think himself back in Hyde Park or Regent Street if

he were to see the dignitaries in their brocade vests, coats of goldlace, broad ruf-
fled sleeves, three-cornered hats and powdered wigs promenading down Queen
Street or going to meeting at King's Chapel or gathering at the Rose and Crown
for a discussion of the latest news and politics.

Perhaps you will be interested in reading of some of the details I have learned
about my predecessors in the collector's position. The first was Mr. Edward Randolph, who was sent here by King Charles II in 1681. I'm afraid he did not make
himself very popular when he immediately upon arrival posted an advertisement
in the town house to inform the people of the new office he was establishing. In
fact, the general court of the day forced him to tear down the advertisement, and
they used great effort to keep him from doing his work. He must not have been
entirely bad, though, since they say he established the first Episcopal church here.
While this is very pleasing to me, it does not please the Puritan element in the
least. Along with his abrogation of the colony's charter in 1684 and his resolute
manner of collecting revenues, building that church made him exceptionally
obnoxious to a certain segment of the people. They had a rather quaint name for
him. They called him "the myrmidon of a tyrant", and once William and Mary
took the throne in 1688, he was put in prison until he could be sent back to
England. I have to confess it was necessary for me to look up the word 'myrmidon' in my Oxford. It is defined as "a loyal follower, or a subordinate who exe-
cutes his orders without question or pity". I believe it referred to the Thessalian
people who accompanied their king, Achilles, and followed every order he issued
during the Trojan War. While the men who work for me are for the most part
loyal and conscientious, I doubt I will ever be called a myrmidon.

Following Mr. Randolph's arrest, the position was then called the naval office,
and it was held by William Brenton, Esq. I gather he was more acceptable to the
people, although there was once when he was assaulted in public by Sir William
Phipps for some indiscretion, real or perceived by Phipps. I suppose no one can
please all of the people all of the time. John Jekyll, Esq., nephew of Sir Joseph,
was next in line and kept the office until his death at the end of 1731. By all
accounts, he was an honest collector. He was succeeded by his son until March of
this year. Now it is my turn, and I shall be assisted by Mr. William Sheaffe, who
served as collector, pro tem, until my arrival. These latter seem to have had no
unpleasantries with the people, which I suspect may be because of their interpret-
ing the regulations in such ways as to favor American traders. I might be wise to
follow his example.

While the collectorship is considered a lucrative position, the actual salary I
will collect is no more than 100 pounds sterling per year. It is the perquisites that

make the position so attractive. Speaking of money, Massachusetts was the first colony to have its own currency. Unfortunately, they did not stick to just one kind, and there are now several different currencies in use all at once. It is extremely difficult to figure the value of each type, since it changes constantly. There are rumors that we will be eventually forced to return to using just one form of currency. I devoutly pray the rumors prove true.

So, dearest Mother, everything looks quite rosy here, but I have observed some signs of unrest among the less wealthy citizens that may one day erupt into more serious disturbances. They seem to resent some of our King's actions. There is a certain group who chatter incessantly about independence, although I fail to see how they would thrive without the benefits of English leadership.

Mother, I believe I have written so much that you will tire of reading it, and so I shall quit here. It is my plan to give this packet to the captain of a ship which is leaving for London in a few days. I trust it will reach you and that you know that my love for you and others of our family is in every word therein.

Your son,
Charles Henry "Harry" Frankland.

Harry did not mention, because he was quite unaware of the fact, that he was now living a mere twenty-five miles from Miss Agnes Surriage.

CHAPTER 11

▼

Harry Frankland's first official business as collector was to place an order in the "Evening Post", dated December 2, 1741, stating that "coasters must not fail to be entered and cleared at the Custom house as the statute demands." During the week he was kept busy certifying the registry of ships in the harbor of Boston, inspecting cargoes and collecting duties and taxes. On Sundays he regularly attended services at King's Chapel, and contributed generously to the erection of a new church to replace the 1689 wooden building which was in an advanced state of decay. His contribution in 1741 was 50 pounds sterling. Gov. Shirley was said to have contributed 100 pounds, and the wealthy merchant, Peter Faneuil, gave 200 pounds. Harry would make cash and material gifts to King's Chapel throughout his lifetime.

Although life in Boston went on as usual, its citizens were becoming more and more concerned over the sight of French cruisers all up and down the eastern seaboard. Harry could not help but wonder if his brother Thomas would some day be involved with them. He hoped Thomas would not be placed in danger, but supposed that was exactly what Thomas himself most yearned for.

By the summer of 1742, the people of the Massachusetts Bay colony were concerned enough about the French cruisers that they feared some sort of attack might be forthcoming. The town of Marblehead, twenty-five miles north of Boston, was authorized to build a fort to defend its harbor, which, at that time was second only to Boston in the volume of commerce it accommodated. Harry Frankland was sent to Marblehead to oversee the construction of Fort Sewall, named in honor of Chief Justice Samuel Sewall, one of Marblehead's most prominent citizens.

This would not be the first fort built in that town. Remains of several palisaded forts left by the Indian population were found around the area. An entire fortified village was discovered on the high ground overlooking Salem Harbor. It was about 25 acres in size and included a low embankment on the edge of the hill, which was about five feet in height with a ditch dug out before it. Numerous depressions within the area, ranging from circles of five to twelve feet in diameter show where the homes of the Indians, known as weekwams (wigwams) were placed.

Harry was not there to look at Indian forts. Fort Sewell was being built in a much different way to defend against a more sophisticated enemy. When his work for the day was completed, Harry and his companions proceeded to the Fountain Inn nearby on Orne Street for some refreshment and more political conversation. It was there that he first met Agnes Surriage.

Agnes was the daughter of a poor, but pious, couple, Edward and Mary Surriage and was born on April 17, 1726. She had spent her early, more carefree years, exploring the delights of Marblehead, which by then was already nearly 100 years old. It had been settled around 1629 by settlers from the islands of Guernsey and Jersey in the English Channel. The town was incorporated on May 2d, 1649. Agnes often stood on the future sight of Fort Sewall to admire the ships in the harbor, or to look across to the almost-island known as The Neck, which was connected to the mainland at the far end of the harbor by a narrow bit of land which separates Marblehead Harbor from the Atlantic Ocean.

Agnes would often run errands for her mother in the shops surrounding the Town House, which was built when she was just one year old. She may have stepped into that building on occasion to look at the deed, written on animal skin, which was signed by Indians of the Winnepawauken, Quonapahkownat and other tribes to transfer ownership of the land to the white men for the sum of 16 pounds, but her favorite recreation in those early days was to take her youngest brother Isaac to the Old Burying Hill, just up the street from the Fountain Inn.

Marblehead had been thoroughly scraped by the glaciers of the Ice Age. Many bare rocks protrude from the thin covering of soil remaining in place in most areas of the town, and these bear scratches and lines left by the glaciers' slow movement across the land. A visitor to the area once asked, "Where do they bury their dead?" It was a good question. There did not seem to be enough earth to cover a body anywhere. However, if one looks closer, he will see that on the sides of the hills or in the valleys between the rocks, there is enough earth for burial. The hill where Agnes and her brother played may have been chosen for the town's first cemetery simply because it was the highest point in the town and the site of the first meeting-house the early residents built for their worship services. The people of Marblehead, as elsewhere throughout the colonies, continued the old English tradition of burying their dead in their church-yard. Not only did this particular hill provide a grand view of the surrounding country and the shore, but it was ideal as a point from which to look out for approaching attackers, whether they were Indians of the area or unfriendly ships approaching from the Atlantic.

Agnes was not much interested in the whys or wherefores, but simply enjoyed playing her version of hide-and-seek with her little brother behind the old tombstones. If Isaac became unruly or fractious, Agnes would quickly settle him down by telling him Old Diamond would get him. Old Diamond was a mixture of fact and folklore in Marblehead that was quite frightening to a small boy. Edward Diamond was born in one of the oldest houses in town. It was commonly referred to as The Old Brig and stood directly opposite the Old Burying Hill where Agnes and Isaac played. Diamond was thought by the townspeople to be a wizard, and the more superstitious fishermen of the town listened in awe to tales of his powers. They were told that when Old Diamond was out at sea, he often sent his crew below decks as darkness approached, telling them he would have other helpers during the night. In the morning, they would be amazed to see the decks piled high with fish, apparently caught by these unseen assistants. Sometimes the men heard Diamond talking above them. He would issue orders to those he called Red Cap and Blue Cap, which were followed to the letter, although the sailors never caught sight of the phantom crewmen. On dark and stormy nights, Old Diamond roamed the Old Burying Hill, beating about among the graves to keep the vessels at sea from shipwreck. Frightening as he might have been to children and superstitious adults, it appears there were times when he had the town's best interests at heart.

If Agnes had been able to read at that time, she might have found interesting some of the oldest grave markers on the hill, those bearing inscriptions such as:

Here lyes buried ye body of Mary wife to Christopher Lattimer Aged 49 years Dec'd ye 8 of May 1681.

Or another which mentions the same Christopher Lattimore, who died at about age 70 in October of 1690.

She would have been amused to read the one bearing a name similar to her own: Agnis Negro Woman Servant to Samuel Russel aged about 43 years dec'd July ye 12 1718.

Or the one with no date announcing: Here lyes ye body of Mrs Miriam Grose who decd in the 81st year of her age and left 180 children grand children and great grand children.

While Agnes enjoyed her visits to the Old Burying Ground, she was almost equally fascinated by the stories her father told about the Indians who once lived in Marblehead and the several sites around that town where Indian burial grounds had been found. Mr. Surriage seemed particularly proud of the fact that more Indian antiquities had been found in Marblehead than in any other place in the entire northeast. Besides burial places, and the remains of the fortified village and two palisaded forts, there was other evidence of the Indian population to be found in piles of shells they had left behind. A line of quarries which supplied the Indians with material to make weapons and other useful implements still existed.

The nearest Indian burial site to Agnes' home was the one overlooking Salem Harbor. It was not the largest (at least two other sites had forty graves in each), but it was one in which Indian skeletons were found in a state of perfect preservation. It was determined that these Indians had died after the coming of the white man, since a variety of articles of foreign manufacture were found with the skeletons. Of course there were no gravestones to mark the resting places of the Indians, who, according to local lore, were buried in a sitting position.

Now, at age 16, Agnes could no longer enjoy the freedom of her younger years. She had no more time to play in the white man's burial ground or to think about the fate of the Indians who once lived in the area. In order to help her family, she was working at the Fountain Inn, scrubbing the floors and stairs. It was there that Harry Frankland first saw the uncommonly beautiful, barefoot, girl in her plain and tattered dress. The aristocratic Frankland had doubtless seen many such girls of a class far humbler than his own, but there was something about Agnes that caught and held his attention. Was it her rich black hair? Or her long-lashed eyes which gleamed with light? Was it the sweetness of her voice when she spoke? Whatever it was, he called her to him and inquired why she wore no shoes or stockings. She replied with beguiling candor that she had none, at which Harry gave her a crown and instructed her to buy some. Harry soon returned to Boston, but the memory of young Agnes Surriage went with him.

Whenever he thought of his visit to Marblehead, he saw once again in his mind the face of the beautiful young woman. In the fall of the same year, Harry again had business in Marblehead. Again he visited the Fountain Inn, and again Agnes was there, still employed to scrub floors and still barefoot.

"Why did you not buy shoes with the crown I gave you?" he asked.

"I did, indeed, Sir, but I keep them to wear to Sunday meeting." Such naivete, coupled with her natural beauty, her lovely form, her artless and modest demeanor, so entranced the aristocratic Frankland that he went to her parents and urged them to allow Agnes to go to his home in Boston as his ward. Her parents, knowing the difficult future facing their lovely daughter, and fearing she would soon find herself married to one of the equally poor boys of the town, agreed.

Harry sought out fine tutors to teach her reading, writing (in which she developed a fine, flowing penmanship, but never quite mastered correct spelling), music, dancing, embroidery and all pursuits enjoyed by young women of the day. So began the transformation of Agnes Surriage into a young woman educated and aristocratic in all but birth. As it had not been during Harry's education, so it was not all work for Agnes during hers. On many an evening she sat by his side embroidering while he read aloud from the "Gentleman's Magazine", the "Spectator" or the "Boston Evening Post", and whenever he drove out to Salem or Marblehead or Cambridge in his carriage, she accompanied him. They played whist or dominoes with Gov. Shirley and his wife Lady Frances from time to time, and Harry was pleased to have this pleasant relationship with the governor despite their competition for the office of collector. By now Shirley no doubt felt getting the governorship was the better deal after all, an idea that would become even more certain in his mind in the next few years.

Harry would leave Agnes at home to pursue her studies when he attended the hunts which were popular with the gentlemen and would always be one of his favorite sports, but she always accompanied him when he took a pleasant trip to Nahant or Marblehead in the custom house boat. Her love of the ocean never wavered.

As the days and weeks went by, Harry found himself more and more often discussing the issues separating England and France and wondering where they would lead. He hoped it would not mean war. Talk of independence was spreading throughout the colony. Harry did not agree with those who favored it and feared they might well bring serious repercussions from England.

Equally disturbing, he found his feelings for Agnes were no longer those of a guardian for his ward. Had she been born of his class, he had no doubt he would marry her, but under the circumstances, how could he? His family name would be ruined, his people would feel betrayed, and even his position as collector might be put in jeopardy. He knew he loved her; he knew he wanted her, yet she was ten years younger than himself, even now just seventeen. Should he speak his feelings to her now, or should he wait another year when she would become of age and no longer need a guardian? He tossed and turned in his bed many a night seeking an answer to his dilemma.

CHAPTER 12

▼

During the next months, Harry, along with all the people of Boston, became increasingly concerned by the presence of French cruisers in the area. Harry alone was concerned with his feelings for Agnes. He was finding it more and more difficult to maintain a guardian-like relationship with his ward, who was growing more beautiful with each passing day. With aching heart he went about his daily business as collector and maintained his generous contributions to King's Chapel, as well as to Harvard College. In March of 1743 colony records show that his work consisted of such mundane chores as certifying that bond had been given relating to the register of the sloop Sea Flower, owned by Benjamin Holt, persuant to act of Parliament. In April that same year he certified that security was given relating to the registry of the sloop Enterprise, Richard Waite, master, at present lost, or mislaid, pursuant to act of Parliament. He would sign many such documents in his large, bold handwriting: H. Frankland, Coll. If it were not for the perquisites of the position, he might well have become bored by such routine duties.

So it was that in the summer of 1743 he was thankful to learn that his beloved brother Thomas would be arriving at the harbor in Boston with the frigate Rose. Thomas had been appointed to the command of this vessel in July of 1740 and had the honor of carrying Gov. Tinker to the Bahama Islands at the end of that year. He had spent two years cruising in that region for protection against the Spaniards, who had joined the French as potential enemies of the colonies. He made a name for himself in June of 1742 when he captured a 20-gun Spanish vessel, a ship armed to match his own Rose. Once again the end of the year proved of great importance in his career, for it was then that he was able to take not only a large Bermuda sloop, but also a Dutch snow, which is a square-rigged ship that differs from a brig in having a trysail mast close abaft the mainmast. Each of these vessels carried a great amount of silver. Now he was in Boston for a long overdue visit with his brother.

The two men embraced heartily at the pier. "That's a fine ship, Captain Frankland," Harry complimented his brother.

"She is that, Harry, even though she's no longer young. I have been told that she first visited Boston well over fifty years ago, back in 1682, I believe it was. She had the honor of bringing the Rev. Robert Ratcliffe here to serve as Boston's first Episcopal minister. But I agree she looks pretty fine for a girl her age."

"So you have achieved your goal of becoming a captain in His Majesty's navy, Thomas. Are you going to aim for Admiral as our good uncle once suggested?"

"At the moment I'm quite content with being a captain, but if more honors come my way, I shall welcome them wholeheartedly, though I'm not sure an admiral would be allowed to have the fun and excitement I've enjoyed."

"I think I envy you that excitement, Brother. I have many things in my life to keep me content, but excitement is not one of them."

"There's plenty of time for that, Harry. Don't give up on it. Mother wrote me that you have a fine house here and a young ward. What is that all about?"

"What don't you understand about a house and a ward, Thomas?"

"Aha, you have not forgotten how to be evasive, have you!"

"Come with me, and I'll show you the house and introduce my ward. Her name is Agnes. Will that satisfy your curiosity?"

"That's a question I cannot answer until after we're introduced."

Harry, thinking it best to refrain from further discussion of Agnes at the moment, led the way to his home. Thomas was suitably impressed and complimented his brother on achieving such a fine standard of living so soon after arriving in the colony. He was not, however, prepared for the beauty, grace, charm and intelligence of his brother's ward.

As they sat in Harry's front parlor after dinner, enjoying fine cigars and imported wine, Thomas could not remain quiet about Agnes. "Harry, my dear brother, I believe I have noticed a certain something in the air when you and the lovely Agnes are in the same room. Are you certain your relationship is no more than that of guardian and ward?"

"I see you have not lost your knack of asking impertinent questions, Thomas. What would give you such an idea?"

"Oh, only the way you look at her and she looks at you, only the deference you give her whenever she speaks. Need I go on?"

"No, I had hoped I was not that transparent. If you noticed in the brief time you have been here, it's possible others have seen it as well. I confess. I love her with all my heart, but what can I do about it? You know as well as I the unwritten laws that govern men of our standing. It would be disastrous to even consider marrying beneath our rank. This has been tearing at my soul for some months now, and I am no closer to a solution to the problem."

"I'm sorry you are in such a state, and I am eternally grateful that the beautiful woman who stole my heart, my darling wife Sarah, was the daughter of Judge Rhett of South Carolina, and therefore acceptable in the eyes of all society. Have you spoken to Agnes of your feelings?"

"How could I? If I told her how I felt and followed that by saying I could not consider marrying her, would I not lose whatever kind feelings she may harbor about me? Would she not lose respect for me and feel demeaned? I would rather go on forever as her guardian than hurt her in the slightest."

"But how long can you remain in that role? She won't need a guardian in a few years. Then what?

"I've tried not to look that far ahead."

"You haven't asked my advice, but when did that ever stop me? Truly, I think you should tell her how you feel and see how she reacts. My intuition about women is rarely incorrect, and it is telling me she feels the same way. She is an intelligent girl. She knows where you came from and where she came from. I suspect she understands the pitfalls of your marrying out of your class. If you can convince her that your love is everlasting and faithful, she may surprise you and live with you without a formal marriage contract."

"Are you suggesting she would be my mistress? How can I ask that of her?" Harry had not considered that possibility and was aghast at the very thought of it.

"Speak to her kindly and lovingly. If she rejects you, apologize, and agree to continue as you are. But if she accepts you, think how improved your life would become. Why you might even find it exciting."

"Along with other of your attributes, I see you have also not lost your late-won mastery of teasing. You are right. I cannot go on this way. I must lay my cards on the table, and soon. Thank you, Thomas. You have helped settle my mind on this question. I will speak to Agnes, and I pray you have correctly diagnosed the situation."

The brothers changed to the subject of the issues between France and England. The following morning, August 22d, the "Evening Post" contained a poem addressed to Thomas. It was written in extremely flowery and hyperbolic rhyme, and offered Harry the opportunity to return some of his brother's teasing, although, in fact, he was quite moved by the final lines of the verse and promised to copy it in full when next he wrote to their mother.

After a pleasant tour of the City of Boston, enjoying his brother's hospitality, and exchanging pleasantries with Agnes, Captain Frankland sailed away the next morning, not knowing what laurels and honors would yet come his way. Harry wished him Bon Voyage and promised to take his advice about Agnes.

That evening, when they had finished their dinner, Harry invited Agnes to join him in the same parlor where he had had his discussion with Thomas. They did not often sit there, and Agnes wondered what was afoot. Harry saw that she was comfortably seated in one of the tapestry-covered chairs then pulled his own chair up beside her. "Agnes, my dear, there are some things of great importance that I need to discuss with you, and they are most difficult for me to express," he began.

"Sir Charles, is something wrong? Are you ill?" She was immediately alarmed by the serious expression on his face.

That response gave Harry a little more confidence. "No, Agnes, I am quite well. I appreciate that that was your first concern." He paused, thinking how best to say what was on his mind. "You have lived here in my home for more than a year now, my dear. Have you been happy?"

"Yes, Sir Charles. How could I not be happy? You have been uncommonly kind and generous to me, and you have provided me with experiences and luxuries I never could have enjoyed had you not rescued me from a life of poverty and want."

"Agnes, if you will allow me, I shall provide these things for you as long as you live." He saw that she did not yet understand what he was getting at and decided it was time to say straight out what was on his mind. "Agnes, my dear, please do not be offended in any way by what I must say. It's simply this. My feelings for you no longer are those of a guardian. They are more like that of a husband. What I'm trying so clumsily to say is that I love you, I want to take care of you and I want you in my life for as long as we live." Harry felt a great weight come off his shoulders. He could almost hear his brother Thomas chiding him, "That wasn't so hard, now, was it?"

"Oh, Sir Charles, how could that be? You are so much above me in society. You could have any one of many beautiful, wealthy, charming ladies." Agnes could not believe what Harry was telling her.

"What you say may be true, my love, but you are the only one I want. Can you possibly have any similar feeling for me?"

She looked into his eyes and said, "Since the day we first met," and blushed, which only added to her loveliness.

"My dear. You make me very happy, but there is yet one more matter for us to discuss, and I pray it will not change your opinion of me. It is the matter of marriage. As you have indicated, I have been born into the aristocracy and am subject to the customs and ways dictated by that society. One of those ways precludes our marriage, as earnestly as I might wish it. I have sought but not yet found an answer to this problem." Harry held his breath for a moment. Would Agnes be offended or angry? Would she leave the room and refuse to speak to him ever again?

She put her hand in his and said, "Sir Charles, I know you to be a man of honor and worthy of the respect of your peers as well as your inferiors. You have declared your love for me, and I return it to you in full. I trust your word completely. If you swear fidelity to me, I will accept that and joyfully live with you as your wife in every way except in law."

"Are you certain you can do this, Agnes? As my brother pointed out, you can pass as my ward for a bit longer, but once you reach your majority, there could be unpleasant talk about our living arrangement."

"I shall ignore it, Sir Charles."

"Then there is just one more thing to settle. You may call me Sir Charles in public, but when we are alone, I wish you to call me Harry. I long to hear my name spoken by your sweet lips, and speaking of your sweet lips, shall we seal our arrangement with our first kiss?"

He rose from his chair and pulled Agnes to him. As she returned his kiss with equal passion and love, he knew he would have no trouble remaining faithful to this lovely woman throughout his lifetime. An idea came to him. Should he suggest it to her? He remembered her words of trust and decided to do so. "Agnes, what would you think of the idea of us having our own private wedding ceremony? Just the two of us? I realize it would not be binding in the face of society or law, but in my mind we would be bound to each other forever."

"Harry, I am already bound to you in my heart, but your idea is a lovely one, and I think we should plan it straight away."

"To me, there's nothing better for our purpose than the marriage rite in my prayerbook. We could kneel together and read it to each other. If you like, and since this is between the two of us alone, I will read the priest's words."

"That sounds wonderful, Harry. Would you mind if I lit two candles? When we finish with the reading, we could join the two flames together to symbolize that we are joining our two hearts and minds and bodies together."

The rite was performed as they planned. It was carried out reverently, sincerely, and in the sight of God, but not the sight of man. When it was over, each confessed to feeling exalted. Harry held her again in his arms and told her, "You have made me very happy, Agnes, and I will cherish you forever."

They talked for a while. When Harry was sure the servants had retired to their rooms on the third floor, he asked, "Are you ready to go to bed, my dear?"

"I'm ready," she replied, "but what of the servants? What will happen if they find that we are sleeping in the same room?"

"You will have noticed that all our staff is mature and experienced. I chose them for those very qualities, and I pay them well. What they see and hear will go no farther than their quarters. They know better than to gossip outside this house. I fear we cannot keep our new living arrangement from them for long, but they will treat us as if their eyes were blind and their ears deaf. I wish it were not necessary for us to keep our new relationship from the outside world, but I have confidence the world will not hear of it from anyone in this house. That is the most assurance I can give you," Harry told her.

"Then I shall get my things from my room and meet you in yours."

As she climbed the stairs to the room she had used since coming to Boston as Harry's ward, Agnes went over in her mind the events of the evening. Could it be true or was she merely dreaming that Harry loved her, that they had exchanged vows of fidelity, that from this day forth they would be living as man and wife? She remembered the solemn way he read from his prayer book, the intense look of love on his face when they joined their lighted candles. It was all true. She wished she could tell her family, but how would they respond? She and Harry felt married in their hearts, but would her family accept their private ceremony? Oh, well, she didn't need to face up to that tonight. When it became necessary, she'd do her best to make them understand. For now, she had only to hug herself in her happiness, pick up her nightgown, her hairbrush and a few other items and make her way quickly to his room, not at all sure what would happen wnen she got there but knowing in her heart it would be something to bring her great and lasting joy.

Soon Harry entered the room and after offering her one last opportunity to reconsider her decision and finding she did not require it, he began to remove his clothing. Agnes watched with interest and anticipation, but he saw a perplexed look cross her lovely face. "What is it, dear?" he asked.

"As you know, I have no knowledge of what to do or what to say, Harry. My mother never spoke of what goes on between married couples, and I had no older sister or older friends who might tell me these things. As you have taught me reading and writing, now you must be my tutor in the ways of love."

Harry laughed happily. "That will be the best tutoring position in the world. Come, I'll show you everything you need to know. As for what to say, simply say, "Yes, Harry" to everything I say or ask."

It took but a second for Agnes to realize he was teasing her. "Yes, Harry," she said, and she laughed along with him. Shyly she reached out to touch him. He pulled her close to his body. She felt new sensations running through every part of her body. What could they mean? What did it matter? They were thoroughly enjoyable. He helped her undress and joined her in the big four-poster bed. Gently and tenderly he showed her the ways of love and was gratified that she learned quickly, surprising him with some ingenuous moves of her own that he had not yet had a chance to teach her. Thus was their love consummated. There was no thought of class or standing. They were united as two equal souls who shared their love in the time-tested way. When they were finished, they knew they had shared a truly spiritual experience, which left them both so exalted that neither could fully express the joy they felt.

So began a new relationship between the lordly Charles Henry Frankland and the lowly Agnes Surriage, cleaning girl from Marblehead.

CHAPTER 13

▼

A few days later, Harry, true to his word to his brother, took up his pen once again to write to his mother. Although he would once again mention Agnes, he was not yet ready to share with his mother the true relationship now existing between himself and the woman she knew only as her son's ward.

"Dearest Mother," he wrote.

"I have recently had a most delightful visit with our Thomas. You must be as proud of him as I am. Just think, he has already attained the rank of captain and has been successful in his first encounters with enemy vessels. I foresee great things for him. I confess to a bit of envy for the excitement in his life. While I have no cause to complain, there is a sameness to my days that makes one indistinguishable from another. Fortunately, my ward, Agnes, is always here to lift my spirits. She has proved to be a charming companion at home as well as when we visit my business colleagues and friends. I believe Thomas found her to be as much a lady as his own new wife.

"I promised my dear brother I would copy for you the entire verse printed in his honor in our newspaper the day after his arrival here. Much as I enjoy poetry, I found this one to be a bit overblown with the exception of the final lines, which were a well-deserved tribute to our Thomas.

TO CAPTAIN FRANKLAND, COMMANDER OF HIS MAJESTY'S SHIP ROSE, NOW IN BOSTON

> From peaceful solitude and calm retreat,
> I now and then look out upon the great;

Praise where 'tis due I'll give; no servile tool
Of honorable knave, or reverend fool:
Surplice, or red coat, both alike to me;
Let him that wears them great and worthy be,
Whether a coward in the camp, or port,
Traitor in want, or traitor in the court,
Alike reward their cowardice deserves;
Alike their treachery, he who eats or starves,
Or brave by land, or hero on the main,
Alike respect their courage should sustain.
Then let me lisp thy name, thy praise rehearse,
Though in weak numbers and in feeble verse.
Though faint the whisper when the thunder roars,
And speak thee great through all Hispania's shores,
Still safe in port the red coat chief may scare,
Dread of the boys and favorite of the fair,
Still shudder at the dangers of the deep;
To arms an enemy; but a friend to sleep.
We see thee, FRANKLAND, dreadful o'er the main,
Not terrible to children, but to Spain.
With thee, thy dawning beams of glory play,
And triumph in the prospect of the day.
O, let the kindling spark, the glowing fire
Your generous soul inflame as once your Sire;
With him the schemes of tyranny oppose,
And love your country as you hate her foes.

"Mother, I really cannot blame the poet for not signing this. I think Thomas himself was a bit embarrassed by it, yet proud at the same time. I suppose the reference to his Sire meant to our ancestor, Lord Protector Oliver Cromwell.

"I trust this finds you and the other members of our family well, and I look forward as always to another packet from you.

Your loving son, Harry"

As he indicated in his letter to his mother, life for Harry Frankland and his beloved Agnes varied little from day to day. Perhaps there would be a wedding or a funeral to attend and congratulations to be sent to parents of new babies and visits made to the sick, but in general, it was business as usual, interspersed with their ordinary pleasures. Some evenings they sat close together while Harry read poetry aloud. Agnes found she related to Shakespeare's "When Icicles Hang By the Wall." Greasy Joan at her pot and Marian with her red and raw nose, reminded her of her early days in Marblehead. She was much affected by Harry's sensitive reading of poems of love and fidelity.

He enjoyed the poetry of John Donne: "Death Be Not Proud" and "Go and Catch a Falling Star", written over a hundred years earlier. Whenever Agnes praised him for his honorable ways, he delighted in returning with the final words of Richard Lovelace's "To Lucasta, Going Into War"—"I could not love thee, Dear, so much Loved I not Honor more." This so delighted Agnes that she sought every possible opportunity for praising Harry's honor.

Harry was reading one of his newspapers one evening in 1744 and noticed the announcement of a birth to a family in Agnes' home town of Marblehead. He brought it to her attention. "Agnes, my dear, were you acquainted with the Thomas Gerrys when you lived with your parents?"

"Harry, dearest, you do honor me to think I might have known folks of such standing. Captain Thomas Gerry is one of Marblehead's most eminent merchants. You've seen his house. It is across the street from the Old North Church. Of course, I saw the captain in town from time to time, and once he tipped his hat to me. I could barely believe my eyes. He is a very fine gentleman. I remember well one day when I was doing an errand for my mother when a sudden nor'easter came up. I was nearly blown away by the wind, and I was pelted with the hardest rain I ever endured. Captain Gerry happened along in his coach at that time, and he picked me up and drove me to my home. I think my mother was quite frightened to see such a fine gentleman bringing me home. She thought I may have been struck by lightning or some other calamity befallen me. To this day I have the greatest respect for the captain. Not all men of such standing would take pity on one such as I."

"Darling Agnes, not all men are as discerning as Captain Gerry and myself. In any case, the Gerrys have a new son they named Elbridge."[1]

"Oh, I'm so happy for them.

There was something wistful about Agnes' voice as she made that remark. She sat quietly with her hands folded in her lap and her head bowed. Harry looked up from his newspaper and asked what was wrong. He hoped Agnes was not feeling low because she wanted a baby of her own. He was relieved to find that was not the case.

"It's my mother, Harry. Since my dear father died, it has been very hard for her to take care of her house and my younger siblings. Now I find she has used all the money she and my father had saved. Of course, it was not very much, but it is gone now, and she doesn't know how they will get along."

"Do not your older brothers help her?"

"Oh, yes, as much as they can. They bring her flounder and other fish they catch in the harbor and they dig clams on the other side of Marblehead and bring them to her. Sometimes they are given one-claw lobsters or crabs with missing legs by some of the more kindly fishermen at the wharf, and they bring what they can of fresh vegetables, but they have their own families to feed and can spare only small amounts."

"You should have told me she was in such straits, Agnes."

"But, Harry, you have done so much for me, and thereby for my family, that I could not ask you for more."

"My dear, I have more than enough for all of us. How can I help her?"

"Well, you know how proud Mother is. She would not easily accept charity, but you may be surprised to learn that she owns some land in Maine, although it may no longer have much value."

Harry was astonished by that bit of information. "How did she acquire land, Agnes?" he asked.

"It's a long story, and I may not have it exactly right, but from what I remember of her telling me, her grandfather was a man named John Brown, who settled in a place called Pemaquid in Maine soon after the Pilgrims landed at Plymouth. John Brown purchased a large tract of land from two Indian sagamores, Captain John Samoset and Unnongoit. I think Mother told me a sagamore is just one rank below that of chief in Indian tribes. I have no idea how one of them got the name of Captain John. Mother didn't have an answer for that when I asked her."

"Probably the white men gave him that name," Harry offered.

"Anyway, the land was in Lincoln County and was known as the Brown Right. Then Richard Pierce married one of John Brown's daughters, and he purchased land at New Harbor, which is about eight miles north of John Brown's land. Mother said he paid the Indians fifty skins for it. Well, Richard Pierce was my grandfather, my mother's father, and he built a fine garrison house on his land. At that time he must have had some money, because when the war with the Indians started, his son John, my uncle, had a vessel and thirty men take his whole family away from there. That is how my family arrived at Marblehead."

"And I'm so glad they did. I should never have found you in Maine."

"Oh, Harry, I do love you so. But to continue my story, as I understand it, some years later, around 1696, the land owned by both John Brown and Richard Pierce was broken up into smaller parcels and lost most of its value. Even so, several people laid claim to it. That's all I know. I have no idea what happened to it after that, but Mother believes she still owns one-seventh of it."

"I'll look into it, Agnes, and see if there is anything I can do about it."

"Thank you, my love. You are so good to me and my family."

"Should I not be? You know I love you with all my heart. It's only natural that I would want to help those you also love."

"I just wish I could do something for you some day." She could not know then that in another ten years she would repay Harry's kindness many times over.

True to his word, Harry was able to locate information concerning the land in Maine, and in December of 1745 a deed to the property was filed in Suffolk County showing that he purchased whatever rights Mrs. Surriage had to the property. The deed describes the tract of land as follows: "A tract of Maine lands and islands, lying and being at a place called Miscongus, in that part of New England that lyes between Kennebeck River and River St. Croix,—said tract extending from Pemaquid Falls eastward and northward as far as the utmost limits contained in the original Sachem's deeds of said lands, made to my grandfather, John Brown, and father, Richard Pierce, both deceased, which lye at Somerset Cove. Broad Bay, Round Pond, New Harbour, or any other place or places whatever, comprehended within the limits of the aforesaid deeds, being one-seventh part of all said tract, as described and bounded therein, as of right descended to me as one of the heirs at law to the said John Brown and Richard Pierce."

The records show that Harry paid Mrs. Surriage fifty pounds for the land. There is no indication that he ever realized any return from his investment. He simply thought it a discreet way to help the mother of his beloved Agnes.

1. Elbridge Gerry was one of the signers of the Declaration of Independence, Governor of Massachusetts, and Vice President of the United States under President Madison. He died in that office in 1814. The home he was born in was later owned by Captain William Blackler, commander of the boat which took George Washington across the Delaware River on Christmas night in 1778 for the Battle of Trenton.

CHAPTER 14

▼

With the opening of what the colonists referred to as King George's War, Harry Frankland would once more stand in the shadow of his friend Gov. Shirley. It was the governor who amassed some 3000 Massachusetts troops in an expedition against the French fortress Louisburg in Cape Breton county in northeastern Nova Scotia. Louisburg was founded in 1713 by French settlers from Placentia, Newfoundland, and as one might suspect, was named for King Louis XIV. It began as a peaceful, but fast growing, shipbuilding center, eventually to become the capital of the French colony of Ile Royale. However, it did not remain peaceful but became the chief stronghold of the French in all of North America. The colonists had been uneasy for several years, knowing such a fortress existed and seeing French cruisers plying the waters up and down the east coast. The Massachusetts militia and those under Commodore Peter Warren and Sir William Pepperell advanced upon the fortress and brought about its surrender in just forty-eight days, ending on June 28, 1745.

Since Harry's services were required at Boston, keeping up with his revenue work and trying to prevent illegal rum and sugar from entering the port, all he could do was discuss the situation with the gentlemen who assembled evenings at the Royal Exchange Tavern. His part in the Louisburg affair consisted of a rousing farewell speech to the troops as they left and another when they returned home. The citizens of Boston were understandably ecstatic at news of the surrender, and it was reported in the newspapers that Boston was "universally illuminated."

In the summer of 1746 Harry's good friend, now Admiral Peter Warren, and General William Pepperell came home from their success at Louisburg. They arrived on June 24th in the 50-gun Chester, its blue flag flying from her mizzen topmast identified her as a vessel of the Blue. At that time the British navy was divided into three sections, the Red, the White, and the Blue, with the Red being the oldest and most prestigious. Sadly, Harry's Uncle Thomas would not live to see his nephew and namesake, Harry's brother Thomas, become Admiral of the White. The Baronet died the following summer, leaving the baronetcy to Harry, since Thomas had no sons, only his two daughters, Betty and Dinah. From that time on Harry was officially known as Sir Charles Henry Frankland, 4th Baronet of Thirsk.

During the festivities in Boston when the Chester was in port, Harry and Agnes may have taken too conspicuous a part. Perhaps they were seen at too many fireworks displays, too many military parades, and too many public receptions. Perhaps they danced too many times together at private parties and balls. Did they sit too close for a guardian and his ward on Captain Alley's packet as it sailed to Lynn? Were they noticed together at events in Salem, Marblehead, Roxbury, Dedham and at Harvard College in Cambridge?

Whatever the reason, their once-secret relationship was found out, and the matrons of Boston were more than a little displeased by it. Harry's aristocratic breeding, his position as collector, and his generosity to King's Chapel were not enough to stop the gossip. The citizens insisted he was not above the moral law. Not even one of Harry's high standing could escape criticism and censure if he indulged in such a living arrangement without benefit of matrimony. By the end of the year, young school children taunted the couple whenever they were seen outside their home.

The couple closed their ears to the clamor raging about them since summer, but Harry knew he must discuss the situation with Agnes.

"My love, I seem to be caught between two unwritten laws. Which way should I turn? I have believed the one law forbade my marrying you; the other condemns me because I did not do so."

"As you say, dear, it would make little difference to those who are eager to find fault in you. Since I am now past eighteen and no longer legally your ward, do you want me to leave your home and return to my mother's home in Marblehead? I could find work and be a help to her. I am more of a hindrance to you here."

Harry was shocked. "Surely you don't believe that, Agnes. A hindrance! It is you who gives meaning to my life. I could not live here without you, and I shall never abandon you so long as I live. You may count on that." Fearing her reply, he had to ask, "Could you really leave me, Agnes?"

"Oh, Harry, I was being foolish. The only way I could leave you would be by death. It's just that I feel it's because of me that you are so harshly criticised."

"We'll face it together, my love, but perhaps we should begin to think of leaving Boston eventually. We could move to the country where we would have more privacy."

"How would you do your work as collector then, Harry?"

"You know my deputy, Mr. Sheaffe, does most of the busy detail work of the position now. I could keep this house and come here whenever necessary to tie up loose ends and handle those things that only I can handle, and sign the papers William prepares for me."

"Where would we go then?"

"Do you remember that lovely little town about twenty-five miles south and west of here that we visited during last summer's festivities? It was called Hopkinton."

"Yes. I thought it so peaceful and rather romantic." Agnes blushed as she spoke those words.

"Then that's the place for us. Just this past Thanksgiving Day my friend at King's Chapel, Roger Price, had enough of battling within the church and resigned his position as preacher. He owned about 700 acres of land in Hopkinton, and I hear he has bought 142 more acres and plans one day to build a new Episcopal Church on it for any who were or would become residents of the town. If things get too difficult here for us, that is where I would want to go."

"Wither thou goest, my dear," she replied and wrapped her arms around his strong body, resting her head on his chest.

He kissed her hair and whispered, "Beloved."

CHAPTER 15

▼

The prospect of one day moving to Hopkinton provided daily conversation material for Harry and Agnes. It kept their minds off the unpleasant and sometimes crude expressions of the citizens of Boston regarding their unacceptable living arrangement. Fortunately, their closest friends, with a few exceptions, stood by them and continued to invite the couple to their homes and accepted invitations to their home for an evening's entertainment.

Harry envisioned a noble house in Hopkinton, set far back from the road with a fine driveway leading to it. The driveway would be lined with stately trees, perhaps it would be cut through an existing forest. The land in Hopkinton was often rolling hills, and Frankland could imagine his house set on the highest part of a many-acre estate. Terraces would be built around the house, and streams would certainly flow through any property he might buy.

"I hope we will have flowers of many different varieties," Agnes said. Harry was in total agreement with her dream. He spent many hours poring over whatever materials he could find concerning what trees, bushes and flowers would thrive in that area, how and where to plant them, and what care they needed. He was especially interested in having fruit trees, apples, pears, peaches, plums, and cherries, which were already found in the colony. He would import apricots and quinces from England. He drew sketches of formal and informal gardens, marking the positions in which he would like to plant boxwood, lilacs, hawthorns and, for Agnes, roses.

"Our place must have a fine, long view," he told Agnes one evening.

"Would we be able to see the ocean?" she asked.

"I'm afraid not, my dear, but the Wachusett and Monadnock mountains are nearby. I shall look for land that faces them. I promise to take you to the ocean as often as possible, but in Hopkinton you may have to settle for streams and perhaps a pond."

"Then we must see that those streams and the pond are well stocked with fish. I am from Marblehead, you know, and I do love seafood. I am not familiar with fresh-water varieties, but I'm willing to give them a try."

"You are a most agreeable lass, Agnes. I promise you will have a home to be proud of. It will be filled with the music you love, and we will entertain extensively. That reminds me, we must have a wine cellar stocked with many excellent European wines, and we shall have to take along my special winecup when we go."

"Which one is that, Harry?" Agnes asked.

"I'll show you." He brought for her inspection a winecup twice as thick as most winecups, so that it would hold only half as much wine as the others. Agnes noticed the small bowl and admired the long slender stem, particularly the crimson-tinted spiral line which ran through the center of it. Harry explained why he used such an unusual cup. "I'm sure you have noticed that it is the custom for our male guests to drink as many drinks as their host. With my special cup, I can drink enough for them to get quite tipsy, while I remain quite in control of my senses."

"Harry, that's not fair."

"Perhaps not, but it is fun. You'd be surprised at the things I learn this way."

They refined their manor plans for several years. It was not until 1750 that Harry's friend Roger Price finally built the church in Hopkinton that he had spoken of so long ago. That same year Harry purchased his first 48 acres of land in that town from a man named Jacob Parker plus another 321 acres "with allowance for highways, as is bounded and described by the plan annexed." The following year he added another 13 acres which he purchased from Benjamin Barnard of Framingham. All of that acreage lies along the slopes of a hill which the Nipmuck Indians called Magunco, "the place of great trees". It is said that John Eliot once had an Indian church on that same property. True to his word to Agnes, this property offered lovely views of the mountains on the northwest, as well as a clear sight of the village of Hopkinton. There were no less than five springlets running down the south and west sides of the hill, combining to form a brook which Nature had stocked with trout.

In 1751 Harry began construction of his dream manor house. It would be large and well-built. The main hall featured fluted columns, and the walls were hung with rich tapestry showing dark figures on a deep green background. Italian marble was imported for the chimney pieces, and all the rooms were finished in expensive decorative materials. Harry acquired slaves to build the terraces he had talked to Agnes about. They also cleared 130 acres of land for tilling, planted the orchards he dreamed of for such a long time, and put up a barn that was 100 feet in length and topped by a cupola. Other buildings on the property included a granary and homes for his servants which were as well built as the homes of the local farmers.

It was 1752 when the couple finally moved to this beautiful new home. Here they expected to spend the remainder of their days. Harry would enjoy hunting for deer in the forests in addition to his much-loved foxhunts. He would catch the speckled trout in Cold Spring brook. Here he would have time to read the literature he could not get to in Boston, the novels of Samuel Richardson, the essays and dramas of Sir Richard Steele, the satire of Jonathan Swift, the essays and poetry of Joseph Addison, once recommended to him by his Uncle Thomas, and the poems of Alexander Pope.

The couple would enjoy entertaining the elite of Hopkinton and Boston in their beautiful home. Agnes would have all the flowers and beautiful music she craved. Harry continued to attend to his duties as collector. A notice he published in the Boston Gazette on February 27, 1753, made known some of the problems he had to face with the smugglers of the period. The notice read: "Boston, Feb. 19th, 1753—Whereas, I am informed there still continues to be carried on an illicit trade between Holland and other parts of Europe, and the neighboring colonies; and that great quantities of European and Asiatic commodities are clandestinely brought from thence into this port by land as well as by sea, and as I am determined to use my utmost endeavors to prevent the carrying on of a trade so prejudicial to our mother country and detrimental to the fair trader, I hereby again give this public notice that if any person or persons will give me information where such goods are concealed, that they may be proceeded against according to law, they, upon condemnation, shall be very handsomely rewarded, and their names concealed; and I hereby direct all the officers of the customs within my district to be very vigilant in discovering and seizing all such contraband goods." This was signed with his usual bold signature, "H. Frankland, Coll."

Their dream of spending years in their lovely home was short-lived. In 1754, Harry Frankland was required to travel to England to take part in a lawsuit against his Aunt Dinah, widow of his Uncle Thomas. The problem was the will of Sir Thomas. In fact, there had been three wills. The first, prepared in 1741, made a minimal provision for Dinah. In another, written in 1744, his widow was to receive the sum of 2,500 pounds per year for life. The last, signed in 1746, left Thomas' entire estate, including all the real estate at Great Thirkleby as well as all of his personal assets, to Dinah, giving her the right to dispose of all of this as she saw fit, without provisions for other heirs at law. It was with a heavy heart that Harry contested the third will. He told Agnes, "It's not that I want Aunt Dinah to leave Thirkleby, but I feel very strongly that the lands belong to the baronetcy, and I must fight to win that consideration. I feel it would be absolutely wrong if she were to leave the property to one of her daughters at her death. The daughter, either Betty or Dinah, could then leave it to whomever she chose. No, I must contest Uncle Thomas's will, as difficult as it is for me to do so."

Harry wrote to Dinah and explained his position. He made it clear to his aunt that she was welcome to live out her life in Great Thirkleby Hall if she so chose, but the land must be transferred to each new baronet at the time the title transferred.

The trip to England was the start of a journey that would forever change Sir Charles Henry Frankland and his relationship to Agnes Surriage. With no forewarning of what lay ahead, the couple looked forward to the trip, anticipating delightful reunions with Harry's people. He was eager to show her Great Thirkleby Hall and its lovely grounds. He couldn't wait to introduce her to his friends. He was certain they would find her as charming and delightful as he himself did. He could not have been more wrong.

Leaving his deputy William Sheaffe in charge of the custom house in Boston, Harry and Agnes left for London, arriving early in the summer. It is difficult to say which of the two was more surprised and distressed by their reception. Harry unfailingly presented Agnes to his proud family with the expectation of a pleasant reception of the woman he loved so deeply. Pleasantry was no part of their response. Agnes was treated to disdain, neglect, incivilities and more. She would later lament that this was one of the worst experiences of her life. One and all made sure she felt totally unwelcome in their circle. Her name was left off invitations to Harry. If he brought her along anyway, the people seated at either side of her at table totally ignored her. If they attended a dance, none of the so-called gentlemen asked her to dance, and when she danced with Harry, the aristocratic ladies gossiped about the couple behind their gloved hands or their fans. Agnes thought how strange that these people of high birth and fine breeding could be so thoughtless of her. The poor fishermen back in Marblehead would have shown more consideration. Her mother's small cottage would have been a far more pleasant place to pass her days. She could not wait to leave these cold, unwelcoming people. How had her beloved Harry sprung from such people as these? Harry did all he could to try to persuade them to accept her. Could they not see that she was the woman he loved? Did they not know it was only because of them and their stiff codes of behavior that he had not made Agnes his wife long ago? Why should she be the one to suffer for his sins?

A special jury was impaneled to hear Harry's case against Lady Frankland in the court of the King's Bench. It took them only an hour and a half to come to their conclusions. They set aside the third will and confirmed the one written in 1744. Lady Frankland would receive her 2,500 pounds per year, but the estate would belong to Harry for as long as he was the baronet. He would see to it that it proceeded to his successor on his own death.

Once the court case was settled, there seemed no further reason to stay in England, especially in view of the cold reception offered Agnes. Sooner or later, most members of the aristocracy made a tour of Europe. Harry felt this was a good time for him to do likewise. He would attempt to make up for the miserable time Agnes had in England by sparing no expense in showing her the sights on the continent. He especially looked forward to visiting Portugal. His long-time friend Henry Fielding had often written to Harry, describing the beauty of the country. He had gone on at length about its sprawling vistas, making the small country seem very large. He wrote of the clear air, wide sandy beaches, rugged mountains. He couldn't get enough of the silvery olive trees, the color-coded trunks of the cork oaks, and the vast vineyards which changed color every season. Fielding had been sure Harry and Agnes would enjoy the wild flowers, the bird songs, the sound of goat bells, and even the occasional sight of a roaming wolf or lynx in the forest or wild boars in the fields. He felt they would thrill to eagles soaring overhead. He promised that the couple would enjoy seeing the old churches and great castles, and villages of stone, but he was even more enthusiastic about the city of Lisbon, exclaiming about the exciting life to be enjoyed there, the gaiety and great wealth, and the lavish receptions and entertainment held for the leaders of society. He often mentioned that the opera in Lisbon was the best in all of Europe.

Harry would be glad to see his friend again. He felt certain Fielding would introduce him and Agnes to Lisbon society and that the couple would be included in the ceremonies associated with the new young King Jose as well as those of the church. Fielding had written that King Jose enjoyed cards, horse-riding and opera and often invited friends to join him in those pursuits.

Harry visualized himself as one of those friends. He could hardly wait to reach the prosperous city of 270,000 citizens rising on the hills beside the Tagus River.

As Harry and Agnes rode from Mattersea to London in a hired carriage with a driver in livery of blue and gold, Harry said, "Agnes, I'm ashamed to say that I have not read some of Henry Fielding's most recent books. We must stop at a bookshop in London and get them. I'll try to read them aboard the ship. It would be embarrassing to meet Henry and have to admit I was ignorant of his works."

"I heard someone say his sister is also an author, Harry," Agnes replied, "I would be interested in reading her books. Do you think we could get them also?"

"Of course, dear. I'm pleased that you would like that. This writing business is a complex thing in many ways. It seems one author works off another to quite an extent. For instance, Samuel Richardson wrote a book called "Pamela; or, Virtue Rewarded". To the best of my knowledge, it was well received, especially by women readers, although Lady Mary Wortley Montagu made a rather disparaging remark about it when she said something to the effect that it was the joy of chambermaids of all nations."

Agnes laughed. "Perhaps Lady Montagu should have tried her hand at writing."

"I suspect she was better at making disparaging remarks," Harry replied. "To go on with this, and I hope I do not bore you with these remarks, Richardson also wrote a book called "Clarissa: or, The History of A Young Lady" some years later. It was only a year or so after Richardson's "Pamela" that Henry wrote "Pamela, An Apology for the Life of Mrs. Shamela Andrews", which was his response to Richardson's book. The next year Henry wrote another book which purports to also be a parody on Richardson's "Pamela". Henry himself called his book "a comic epic poem in prose". That has struck me as a rather grandiose description. He also wrote yet another on the same theme. This was called "Shamella". I don't know how he became so enamoured of this Pamela, Shamella thing. At any rate, I've read all those and admire Henry's writing and wit greatly. I'm sorry to say I never got a copy of his "The Life of Jonathan Wild the Great". I've heard that in it he uses ridiculousness to expose hypocrisy. That seems a popular theme these days, although exposing hypocrisy has not yet eliminated it and probably never will. "Jonathan" is based on the idea that a Great Man brings all manner of mischief on mankind, whereas a Good Man removes mischief. I shall try to get that one for my shipboard reading. It should be interesting to see how he expresses his ideas. I'd also like to purchase "The History of Tom Jones, A Foundling." Those who have read it recommend it highly. I gather the basic theme of it is the nobility of good nature. He wrote me that his newest, "Amelia", was "designed to promote the cause of virtue and to expose some of the most glaring evils, as well public and private, which infest the country."

"The man does have a way with words, doesn't he?" Agnes said.

"Now as to his sister's work, Sarah's first effort, with a preface written by Henry, was "The Adventures of David Simple in Search of a Real Friend." I understand her style is quite different from her brother's. I think it would be an excellent idea for you to read that one and tell me about it so that I can decide if I, too, wish to read it."

"What a good idea, Harry. It can work in the other direction as well. If you think I would enjoy any that you read, please recommend them to me."

"I shall. I think Sarah has a newer book out now with a rather odd title, "Volume the Last". One can only wonder what that is about. Certainly her title does not give away its content. There are other good female writers, Agnes. I think you would enjoy Charlotte Lennox's "The Life of Harriot Stuart" which I have seen touted as more or less a guide to manners and morals in novel form."

"I think my manners are quite satisfactory, thanks to your teaching, and if my morals are not above reproach, that is also thanks to your teaching," Agnes told him with a saucy tilt of her head.

"Your teasing ability is also in good form, dear wife. Lord, I don't know how I became so fortunate as to find you and win your love or how I could have lived my life without you."

Agnes reached over to kiss his cheek and hold his hand.

"You're taking my mind off great literature, you little minx," he told her, "but I do have one last recommendation for you. It is Charlotte Lennox's "The Female Quixote; or, the Adventures of Arabella". It's the story of an aristocratic young woman isolated on her father's estate way out in the country. I suppose for lack of anything else to do, she reads French novels to occupy her time and her mind. Unfortunately, she doesn't always interpret these books correctly and becomes confused about many things, notable among them, men."

"That would not be difficult to do, Harry. Men are a completely different breed from us women."

"And I am most thankful for the differences."

"I, too."

CHAPTER 16

▼

It was almost the end of the year when the couple arrived in Lisbon, and Harry learned that his friend Henry Fielding had died on October 8. This saddened Harry, but even without his friend's presence, the city totally captivated him. He was not particularly impressed with the architecture of the city; it contained an eclectic assortment of styles from periods as far back as medieval times. However, he did find the large open space by the river attractive. It was flanked by the Royal Palace and several government buildings, reminiscent of buildings along the Thames in London. Agnes was reminded of Marblehead when they visited the waterfront. She thoroughly enjoyed looking at the large ships docked there. The skyline was pierced by the steeples of over forty churches, and the rooftops of ninety convents. Harry agreed with a Frenchman who had told him some years earlier that Lisbon was dark and dirty, but nonetheless charming. One could buy fresh fish at the market the man touted as the best anywhere, and the meat market was surprisingly clean. Harry was interested in learning more about the glazed tiles and the unusual pink marble he saw on many of the buildings. The marble was subject to cracking, but appeared to be quite durable in spite of this.

Harry found it difficult to decide whether the city was merely exciting and gay or whether it crossed the line into dissolute, but whatever the case, its wealth, much of it from the huge quantities of gold brought in from Portugal's possessions in Brazil, and the splendor of the capital, had drawn many English merchants there for reasons of trade or health or simply for pleasure. The palaces and churches were filled with expensive art and sculptures; the libraries contained thousands of books; costly merchandise was piled in wharves and warehouses. Portugal had had an alliance with Great Britain since 1703 which allowed Portugal to buy English wool and England to buy Portuguese wine. It was said by some that the wine from Porto was first brought to England in the early 1600's. At first it tasted dry and harsh to the British, then in 1676 two sons of a Liverpool wine merchant added brandy to it and created the first port wine. Port wine played such an important part in English history that some joked that the American Revolution might not have been fought if the English rulers had just not drunk their bottles of port in front of the colonists who had none.

It was not only the wine that made Harry confident he would fit into Lisbon society. He became so enamoured of the city that he would one day write to King George and ask to be made consul general to Portugal.

First, however, he needed to rent and furnish a house suitable for entertaining the members of society he would soon meet. He and Agnes expected to enjoy all the gaiety Fielding had written about. He rented a house from a Mr. Coles at the monthly rental of 32 pounds and settled in. Agnes was pleased that she had a view of the ocean from the grounds of her new home, although it was partially obstructed by churches and trees.

Harry's new journal*, begun in 1755, gives many insights into the life he and Agnes lived in Lisbon. His entries range from deep philosophical observations to notes about his wigs, his clothing, recipes, and his various trips to other parts of Portugal and to England. Although he had decided to make his home in Lisbon for an extended time, he had not lost interest in the events back in the Massachusetts Bay Colony. It bothered him that the colony was in such a state of confusion that, in his opinion, nothing worthwhile could be accomplished. He was quite aware that the French had built a series of forts along the Great Lakes and the large rivers in America, all the way to the Gulf of Mexico and that they were edging into the land occupied by the English on a daily basis.

The thirteen colonies held a meeting in Albany in June of 1754 to come up with a plan against France. Benjamin Franklin proposed that the general government of the colonies would be administered by a grand counsel chosen by the representatives of the colonies. This proposal failed because the colonies were afraid of losing some of their rights and because the king thought it gave them too much power. Frankland felt that the proposal would have made the union of the colonies a powerful entity and that the rights of each colony could be preserved without infringing on the rights of any other colony. He was disappointed when the proposal was defeated, but he may well have taken the advice found in his journal in March of 1755: "In all thy desires, let reason go along with thee; and fix not thy hope beyond the bounds of probability, so shall success attend thy undertakings, and thy heart shall not be vexed with disappointments."

March was a busy month for the baronet. Entries in his journal show that on the 19th he went to Sagavan with a Mr. Horne, on the 21st to a Mrs. Brown's to see a procession, on the 23d he rode on horseback to Don Pedro's Infanta, and on the 27th he was at the court to witness the annual custom of the king washing the feet of poor men. Agnes accompanied him whenever it was appropriate. Surely she was with him on April 1 when he returned from a visit to Colares in the beautiful valley near Cintra, some twenty miles from Lisbon. Colares was known for its excellent wine, and Harry was known for always having excellent wines on hand wherever he lived. On the 5th of that month they drove to Cintra. It was situated at the foot of a rocky mountain and was a favorite summer resort for the rich merchants of Lisbon and the nobility. Its 4,000 inhabitants enjoyed magnificent views of the valley of Colares, the Atlantic Ocean, and the great monastery at Mafra, built between 1717 and 1735 for King John V. This was designed by the German architect Johann Ludwig, and Harry was told that it took 45,000 craftsmen, stone masons and laborers to build it.

Music remained an important part of the couple's lives. In April that year, they attended two operas, and his journal notes he paid "For singing man" 480 crowns. Several recipes for various medicinal potions are found in his journal, indicating that the couple was not immune to the common ailments of the general public. Again, it is hoped he took his own advice at these times. He wrote: "Terrify not thy soul with vain fears; neither let thy heart sink within thee from the phantoms of imagination."

In a more domestic vein he gave directions for white washing: "Take some best stone lime in an earthen pot, to which put a little water and some common Lisbon oil, with some blue. The lime must be put into the water by little and little lest it boil up and hurt the eye."

Ever the consummate aristocrat, he went to the Visconde de Ponte de Limas at Mafra, a shady tree-lined place of 1000 inhabitants about five miles northwest of Lisbon. John V built a palace there which was completed in 1742 and called the Escurial of Portugal. It had 807 rooms, 5200 windows, and was 770 feet in length. The library alone was 300 feet long and at one time contained 30,000 books. Harry described the entrance as having fine marble statues of several saints. The infirmary, he wrote, "is very neat with Dutch tile." The king and queen's private chapel was of marble with grand altar pieces done by Ignatio de Olievira. Harry was particularly impressed that one of the king's coaches cost 120,000 crowns and that the king had nearly 80 coaches in all.

On June 3rd of the same year, Harry took passage aboard the Hanover packet which sailed for Falmouth at 7 p.m. He arrived in England on the 16th and attended to business in Fareham, Exeter, and London, beginning his return trip to Lisbon on September 4. He reached his home in Lisbon just a few weeks before the earth-shaking climactic event of his life.

* Frankland's journal was presented to the Massachusetts Historical Society on October 29, 1851, by Matthias Ellis, Esq., of Boston, and quotes from it were found in "Sir Charles Henry Frankland, Baronet; or Boston in Colonial Times" by Elias Nason, published in Albany, NY in 1865.

CHAPTER 17

▼

On the morning of November 1, 1755, All Saints Day, Harry Frankland got up a bit earlier than usual. The holiday was celebrated extensively by the Roman church in Lisbon, and Harry wanted to see for himself the streets crowded with carriages, the citizens in their finest outfits, all the city's priests, nobles, tradespeople, military personnel and slaves, moving towards the churches to attend high masses. Miss Coles, daughter of the Franklands' landlord, had expressed her wish also to witness the event, and Harry promised to take her along with him. Since Agnes was not fond of crowds, Harry would be pleased to have Miss Coles' company. Hannah, one of the two servants he and Agnes had brought with them from Hopkinton, made him a hearty breakfast, and Robert, their other servant, was asked to get Harry's carriage and horses ready for the ride to church. "Be sure everything is quite clean, Robert; as we wouldn't want Miss Coles to get dust on her dress,." Harry told him. The young woman would soon experience events far worse than having dust on her dress, but there was as yet no hint of the impending disaster.

Agnes planned a pleasant morning at home. It was a warm day for November, and the sun cast a golden glow over the roofs and spires of the city. The sky was clear and bright, the air quiet. The sails of vessels at the docks hung limply by their masts. The waters of the Tagus, which was some three miles wide near Lisbon, were as smooth as that of a small pond. By ten o'clock, the church bells were done with their merry clanging, and most of the people were kneeling in the pews as the services got under way. Nobody could have imagined it was the calm before a storm that would literally destroy the whole city.

Agnes planned to sit in her garden and watch the tiny scrap of the Atlantic that was visible from there. Harry dressed carefully, putting on a newly powdered wig and his best red frockcoat. He went to the garden to kiss Agnes and was pleased when she remarked that he was looking especially elegant that morning. "Is all this for Miss Coles?" she teased.

"Agnes, you know she's much too young to interest me," he replied. She reminded him that she had been even younger when he first met her back in Marblehead.

"But she is not nearly as beautiful as you were then or are now," he responded gallantly with a twinkle in his eye.

"Ah, my love, I see you are as adroit as ever," Agnes said and kissed his cheek. "Now, run along. You musn't keep your young lady waiting."

"She's not my young lady, I tell you. In any event, we won't be long. You enjoy your time by yourself."

"I'll be here when you get back. Be safe, my love," she told him, and he climbed into the carriage and was off to pick up his passenger.

Harry's carriage had just passed the house of one Francesco de Ribeiro when the first of three profound tremors shook the city of Lisbon and was felt as far away as France, Switzerland, North Italy and across the Mediterranean in northern Africa.

"What's happening?" Miss Coles asked in alarm. The whole earth was rising and falling like the waves of the ocean. Buildings were swaying and collapsing, and the steeples of churches crashed to the ground. Before Harry could reply, their carriage overturned, and their horses were instantly killed. Harry threw his body over his companion's in an effort to protect her, but Miss Coles was badly hurt and in such agony that she bit through the sleeve of Harry's red coat, his shirt, and the flesh of his arm. She and Harry had been thrown back into the carriage when it overturned, and Harry was knocked unconscious for a few minutes. Awaking, he asked, "Miss Coles, are you all right?" There was no answer. He realized he had landed on top of her. Getting off, he saw that her eyes were rolled up into her head. He checked for a pulse in her neck and found none. "My God," he cried.

Realizing he could do nothing for Miss Coles, he knew he needed to get out of the carriage, but how? The carriage had arranged itself in such a way that he could see no way out. The window, now at the top, was shattered, and he removed one of his boots and knocked out the remaining glass with its heel. Dust and debris fell onto him. He shook it off and sat for a moment, taking stock of his situation and trying to devise a plan of escape. Although there was dust everywhere, he could breathe. As far as he could tell, he had no serious injuries, only bruises and a cut on his left hand, which he wrapped with his handerkerchief. A large wooden structure lay over the window he had opened, and he found it impossible to move it from inside the carriage. All he could do was pray to be rescued.

The first tremor was followed by two others not more than a minute apart, and the great city of Lisbon lay in ruins. Streets were clogged with rubble. The screams of the injured could be heard all around. Houses, churches, and even the king's palace were destroyed. Fortunately, the king and his family were in nearby Belem at the time, and he would later write to his sister, the queen of Spain, "Here I am, a king without a capital, without subjects, without raiment." People were running in all directions and children ran screaming from their homes. Animals moaned in agony. After the third shock, thick dust settled over the city, and it became as dark as night.

Agnes, back at their home, heard the rumbling sound and could see buildings falling everywhere. Her own house shook and wavered before the roof caved in. She would worry about her belongings later, her first thought now was for Harry's safety. She called Hannah and Robert to come with her to help find him. The two servants had run to the cellar at the first shock and refused to come out. Agnes was frantic, afraid they would be entombed in debris, but she did not have time to argue with them or to get them out of the cellar. Harry could be in great danger. She headed down the hill in the direction he would have taken. She could not at first believe a church would be damaged by an act of God, but she soon passed several that had sustained great damage. As she caught a glimpse of the Tagus River from time to time, she saw the waters rising in great waves over its banks, breaking resoundingly on the shore. She knew many people must have lost their lives these last few minutes and prayed Harry was not one of them.

"How will I find him?" she thought. All she could do was follow the path he usually took when he went to that part of town. This was made difficult by debris and the collapse of landmarks that would have shown her the way. She searched frantically. She saw no sign of Harry, but she would not give up. Ahead she caught a glimpse of a fallen carriage that was the color of the one Harry rode in. Could it be his? Could he have survived the disaster? She called his name loudly, "Harry, Harry Frankland, are you near?"

Harry had been under the debris for nearly an hour when he heard Agnes' voice. At first he thought he was delirious and imagining things, but then he heard her call him again. Were his prayers to be answered at last? During this terrible hour he remembered every sin he had ever committed and wondered if this was God's way of punishing him. As he prayed, he promised that if he were rescued, he would become a better person. He would make things right with Agnes. That would be his first effort to atone for his shortcomings. It no longer mattered to him if his people rejected her or if she was of lower rank than he. He would marry her. He should have done so long ago. He would correct the wrong he had done to the woman he loved with all his heart, if only he would be rescued in time.

Not at all sure it really was Agnes calling, Harry shouted out, "Over here, Agnes. I'm over here. Follow my voice if you are truly there, as I pray you are."

"Harry. I'm here. I can hear you. Are you all right?"

"I'm alive at least, but I cannot move from this place."

"I'll get you out, Harry." She looked at the heavy materials crushing down on his carriage and wondered how she could ever remove them. She saw three men nearby. She offered them large sums of money, and they agreed to help her. They began removing rubble from the area with Agnes working feverishly beside them. She talked to Harry all the while to keep him alert and to bolster his spirits. "It's a terrible sight out here and dark as well, but I promise I'll get you out," she told him.

Harry told them Miss Coles was dead, and they informed him that his horses also had been killed. Aftershocks continued to shake the earth for another twenty minutes. Huge waves lifted in the ocean, pulling the water of the Tagus into the sea, leaving the limp-sailed vessels momentarily on dry land. Then the water rushed back in, smashing the ships and sweeping away the crowds of people who had gathered on the once-beautiful marble wharf. Soon the quay itself was washed into the river. They would learn later that the lovely new opera house, of which all Lisbon was so proud, was no more, and over thirty once elegant churches were destroyed, along with hundreds of homes and shops.

With no shovels, no ropes, nothing but their bare hands, Agnes and the men worked with frantic strength and zeal. Finally, she could see Harry. This gave her more strength. She worked harder and faster. "Can you help us by pushing on that piece of wood, Harry?"

"I'll try. I don't have room to get much of a purchase on it, but I'll do my best. On the count of three."

She and the men pulled and Harry pushed. With great effort they were able to move the heavy beam, and Harry could move freely. They helped him out and took him to the nearest partially standing building, where they tended to his bruises and scrapes. He thanked the men for their help and paid them what

Agnes had promised them, thankful for his habit of carrying fairly large amounts of cash with him wherever he went. He held Agnes as if he would never let her go. "I owe you my life, Agnes. I would surely have soon died under that rubble. I don't know how you ever found me. It seems like a miracle to me, and I shall do my best to repay you as long as I live."

"You owe me nothing, Harry. Don't you know you are my whole life. Without you I would have no life. Finding you was no miracle. It was simply what I had to do."

"Well, I shall be eternally grateful to you, as I have been grateful to God for bringing you into my life and grateful to you for all your years of patient and loving devotion. I only regret that my aristocratic pride stood in the way of my doing what I should have done as soon as we declared our love for each other."

"And what is that, Harry?"

"I should have married you then. Will you forgive me and allow me to make up for my stupidity? Agnes, will you do me the honor of becoming Lady Frankland?"

She had never felt wronged by their living arrangement. She loved him and he loved her. Nothing else was important to her. Now he was proposing marriage to her. Did he mean it, or was it simply the result of his being shaken by the ordeal he had just suffered? The look in his eyes as he waited for her answer, told her all she needed to know. She thought back to the first time they made love and the words he had told her to use whenever he made a suggestion. She smiled at him and said, "Yes, Harry", wondering if he would remember those words.

He remembered. They stood there in the wreckage of a once-great city and laughed. "How could I have been such an idiot? Why, oh, why did I not marry you years ago?" He would later write in a new journal, "We should endeavor to pacify the divine wrath by sorrow for past neglects and a future conscientious discharge of our duty to God and our country."

After a brief rest, Harry and Agnes felt they must try to get to their home to see if Robert and Hannah were buried in the basement or if they had managed to survive. As they made their way around piles of rubble, they saw the first fires. In the end, the many fires would do more damage to the city than the earthquake itself. They passed many people with dazed looks on their ashen faces. Some were crying loudly, others silently. Everyone had a story to tell of their own personal losses. They learned that the prisoners in the jails had been let out and that some soulless citizens had already begun looting deserted buildings. Agnes could scarcely believe anyone would be that base. Rumors of the number of deaths that day were passed from one person to another, each one adding a few thousand to the number. The rumored numbers reached 30,000, but the true number was never known for certain.

It was hours later when they arrived at their home or what was left of it. They were relieved to see Hannah and Robert sitting on a pile of chimney bricks in the garden where just a short time ago Agnes had enjoyed her view of the ocean. It was, of course, impossible to hire a coach and horses. They could not have made their way through the debris-clogged streets if they had one, so Harry and Agnes, Robert and Hannah spent the night in the garden, believing what was left of the house itself was too unstable to stay in. They would salvage as many of their belongings as they could the next day and try to get to Belem, a town about a mile outside Lisbon. They had heard that many refugees were going there. The king's family had been in Belem when the earthquake struck, and fearing more tremors, they chose to stay in tents for several months until a large quadrangular wooden building with twenty-five windows on each side, could be built to house them. People poured into the area, rich and poor alike. Some people whose homes had been spared chose to live outside in makeshift tents rather than stay in their houses, either in fear of more damage or in sympathy with those who had no homes to stay in.

Since the average November afternoon temperature in Lisbon is in the 60's, Harry and Agnes were fairly comfortable sleeping outside that first night after the earthquake. Robert had picked through the rubble and found some tattered and gritty blankets to cover them. They were saddened that their home was badly damaged, but grateful to be able to spend the night in its yard. Soot and dust covered the grass, but they knew it was safer outside than it would be staying inside the house. Harry had checked it carefully and was afraid some of the standing walls were about to cave in. For the moment, at least, they could put out of their ears and eyes the sounds and sights of torment taking place in the city, although nothing could erase the smell of smoke from the many fires that burned throughout the night. As they said their good-nights, Harry promised Agnes that the worst was over and that better days were coming. Tomorrow would be soon enough to deal with all the matters that lay before them. Tomorrow they would leave Lisbon.

CHAPTER 18

▼

Neither Harry nor Agnes slept well the night of the earthquake. Harry, of course, was stiff and aching from the scrapes and bruises acquired during his ordeal under the debris. He could not get out of his mind thoughts of how close he had come to death and how nearly miraculous it was that it was Agnes who saved him. He would not forget the promises he made to God during that time. He would strive to be a better person from that day forward, and he would marry Agnes as soon as he could find a clergyman to perform the rite.

When morning came, their first problem was finding food and water. Robert picked his way gingerly through the rubble to where he thought the food storage area would be found. He was not surprised to find that nearly everything had been destroyed. Flour and sugar had spilled all over the floors, milk and butter were covered with dust and debris. There was a ham that survived, but no way to heat it. The best he could come up with were a few pieces of fruit, not in the best condition, but edible. They ate it quickly and, as quickly, decided they must leave that house. Harry felt their best plan was still to try to get to Belem.

There seemed to be no other way of getting to their destination except by foot, so they could take only absolute necessities with them. They stashed away in what they hoped was a safe place the few items they found intact among the rubble. They took with them the few pieces of fruit they had not eaten the night before. Agnes felt she had never before been so hungry, not even back in Marblehead where food was never plentiful for her family. As they began their journey, they found others headed in the same direction. Little by little they were able to piece together the results of the earthquake. Apparently, one of the worst shocks occurred along the river's north side and did extensive damage from Lisbon some six or seven miles to a point halfway to Sacavem. Extending inland well over a mile, it damaged many churches, totally ruined hundreds of houses and killed hundreds, if not thousands, of people. Among the few buildings that escaped serious damage were the Mint and the English Church.

They learned that certain buildings that might have survived the quake were ruined by the fires. These included the Royal Palace, the Opera House, the Patriarchal Church and many other important buildings. Twenty to thirty parish churches and some of the largest convents of Lisbon were destroyed. Some residents claimed the building that housed the Inquisition was the first to go. That claim has been disputed, but, first or not, the building fell to the ground. In the end, it was ordinary houses and shops that suffered the most, being shattered beyond repair.

The terrible fires burned nearly a week and wiped out the whole of the central part of the city as well as those parts built on the adjacent hills. Winds blowing in from the northeast only made things worse. This would prove to be the worst disaster in the history of Europe, leaving a once proud and prosperous city nothing more than a blackened mess, many of its citizens lying dead beneath the ashes.

Not only buildings suffered during that week. Again, much may have been recovered if it had been only the earthquake, but the fire was voracious in its appetite. In the churches, palaces, and fine houses, pictures of great value, antique furniture, tapestries, china and extensive collections of great books were lost. Merchandise in the shops—silks, silver, china—destroyed. In the palace of the Marques de Lourical, north of the worst of the fire, over two hundred pictures including works of Titian, Correggio and Rubens were lost, 18,000 books, 1,000 manuscripts damaged, including a history book written by hand by the Emperor Charles V and a book of herbs and medicines that once belonged to King Matthias Hunyadi of Hungary (1440-90). Family archives, a collection of maps and charts concerning the Portuguese discoveries and colonization in the East and in the New World burned, as well as seventy thousand books in the King's palace. Several libraries containing books over two hundred years old were ruined.

Refugees Harry and Agnes passed on their way to Belem told of the horror they had witnessed on the Tagus River. At eleven o'clock, great waves poured over the shore, tearing ships from their anchors and washing away all buildings on the quay. Some of these waves were fifteen to twenty feet high. Three times they battered the shore, wreaking their worst violence on the Sao Paulo district and the Terreiro do Paco. The Customs House was greatly damaged and the beautiful new quay built by John V was completely destroyed, carrying somewhere between one hundred and nine hundred people who had assembled there, into the river to drown. They had mistakenly thought that would be a safe place. Once the sea had its fill of bodies and wrecked vessels, it calmed down, the river was again quiet, and by two o'clock, boats were carrying survivors across the Tagus, the water's violence over but never to be forgotten.

While the true number of dead may never be known, they died in hospitals, churches and other places one might have thought to be safe. Strangely, the foreign commercial population of Lisbon suffered far fewer losses, the British Factory being especially fortunate.

Harry and Agnes saw that people crawling out of the wreckage were hurt far worse than Harry had been. They were bleeding profusely, had broken legs and arms. They were crying for help to find family members. Animals were not left unscathed. There were dead and injured horses, mules and dogs along their way. It was feared that the powder magazine in the Castle might blow up at any minute. Patients from the Hospital Real were left outside, little groups of refugees from fallen houses camped near them, and everywhere priests roamed, hearing confessions and giving absolution. Like Harry and Agnes, huge crowds were trying to get out of the city to reach the open country.

In all the horror were a few moments of mild humor, such as when the English clergyman, who did not speak Portuguese, was baptized by Portuguese priests. There were stories of heroism as well. A young lieutenant and four soldiers remained at their posts to protect from fire and looting a large store of gold recently arrived from Brazil. Most parish priests stayed near their churches, and most nuns stayed in the ruins of their convents. Military personnel were called in to help with burying the dead and to maintain order. Able-bodied men were called back into the city to begin the cleanup and, eventually, the reconstruction. Food and other necessities were brought in and made available at stalls set up around the city.

Harry and Agnes at last arrived at Belem where they found the King and his family living outside in makeshift lodging rather than risk being inside their royal residence in case it, too, might crumble. They joined the throngs of refugees making do in tents made of matting, planks and sail-cloth. November 1 was not the end of the earth's shaking. There were many brief aftershocks that did little or no damage, but there were nearly thirty frightening tremors the first week, including one extremely violent one on November 8 and a particularly alarming one on the morning of December 11. One on the 21st of December prompted the British Ambassador in Madrid, Sir Benjamin Keene, to ask, "Will your Earth never be quiet?"

In the next ten months there may have been as many as five hundred aftershocks. Harry Frankland would not stay around to witness them. He and Agnes and their faithful servants would leave for England on the first available ship. He was proud to learn that the British Parliament sent 100,000 pounds sterling as well as food and tools to Lisbon, but he would not be present to see the beginning of the rebirth of the once great city. Before he would leave, however, he would marry Agnes Surriage. The only clergyman they could find at the encampment was a Roman Catholic priest. That mattered little to the couple. The rite was performed, and Agnes, cleaning girl from the Fountain Inn in Marblehead, was at last Lady Frankland, wife of the wealthy baronet she had loved for so long. "My dear," Harry told his new bride, "I never thought to spend my honeymoon in a refugee camp, but I promise things will get better and soon."

CHAPTER 19

▼

Life in Belem was a far cry from the luxury Harry Frankland was used to all his life. Even Agnes' early days in Marblehead were less primitive than the situation she now found herself in. She got through the days by reminding herself that these were temporary quarters, they would soon get out of Portugal, and, most important of all, Harry was safe. She smiled to herself whenever she remembered that she was now Lady Frankland. She wished her mother could know.

Harry went into Lisbon daily, seeking a way to get Agnes away from these deplorable conditions. Occasionally, he would get a ride in a carriage headed into the city from some area not touched by the earthquake, but most days he walked. Every new aftershock strengthened his determination. At last he was able to bring home good news to his wife. He had secured passage for them aboard a ship leaving for London in just two days' time.

"I was able to get a cabin in the roundhouse, Agnes. That is unbelievable luck with so many people trying to get away. I believe God is smiling upon me because of our marriage," he told her.

"I, too, smile whenever I pinch myself and am reassured it is not merely a dream and that I truly am Lady Frankland," Agnes told him and kissed him happily. "But, Harry, may I ask you a very personal question?"

"Of course, you are my wife. I have no secrets from you. What do you wish to know?"

"I cannot understand how you are able to pay for our passage and the supplies you have brought here this past week. The banks are closed, most of the shops are destroyed. It is a great puzzle to me how life continues under these conditions."

"Well, my dear, you must have noticed that I always carry a substantial amount of funds on my person wherever I go. Fortunately, I persisted in that habit on the fateful day of the earthquake. The funds were still in my purse inside my frockcoat when you so kindly disinterred me. Don't you remember that I was able to pay those gentlemen who so ably helped you rescue me? Beyond that, I am well connected in Lisbon, and my acquaintances in all areas of society there are quite willing to accept my notes. They know they will be repaid in due time. It is very difficult for the ordinary people of the area, but quite simple for those of higher rank. I do not by that statement mean to sound elitist. It is simply a matter of fact. It is my firm intention to donate substantially to those devastated by events when we return. I shall make arrangements through my London solicitor. Any other questions, dear one?"

"Just one. What shall we wear on the ship? We have been in these same garments for days on end. They are hardly suitable for our time on board ship."

"I think you will find there are others aboard with the same problem. They will understand and overlook our shortcomings in matters of dress. I promise that we shall go on a fine shopping spree once we are on England's noble soil."

"I shall look forward to that, Harry, much more than I look forward to revisiting the people I met on my last trip to England." Harry was touched by the wistful look on her beautiful face.

"I promise things will be different this time. I take full blame for the discomfort you endured before. I feel certain it was all because I had not had the sense to marry you sooner. Surely, those who treated you so badly could not have found you personally wanting in any way."

Agnes did not reply but hoped with all her heart that his evaluation was correct. It was not in her nature to hold a grudge or be vengeful, and she was quite ready to accept any kindnesses that might come her way from previously rude and discourteous people. She did not, however, wish to repeat the humiliating experiences of that time.

Early in the morning of the day their ship was to leave for London, Harry and Agnes dismantled their makeshift home. Deciding to make a completely new start to their married life, they distributed the few belongings they had brought to the camp area to others who needed them. It was little enough, but the recipients were grateful for anything useful or edible.

As they boarded the ship, Harry seemed deep in thought, and Agnes inquired as to the reason. "I was thinking of something my father said to me just before I left Bengal. He told me he had made the trip in the opposite direction and that it had been made more pleasant because he was accompanied by his wife, my mother. I have made many trips in my life, but I look forward to this one more than any other because I, too, will be accompanied by my dear wife."

"Even in her one soiled and tattered dress?" Agnes teased.

"In or out of it, my love."

Agnes blushed as they approached their cabin. Once more Harry flashed back to that first voyage. "You know, when I saw my cabin in the roundhouse for the first time, all I could think of was that it was nowhere near as comfortable or luxurious as the home I was leaving. My dear Uncle Arun chided me on that, saying I was very fortunate to be able to stay in the very best accommodations aboard. Now it occurs to me that these same accommodations are far superior to the ones we have just left. Once again, it has been proved that one's values often depend on one's circumstances."

"Well, I have rarely found circumstances inferior to where I came from, except our last home."

"I would not exactly call our latest accommodations 'home' except for the fact that home is where the heart is, and my heart is ever where you are."

"My dear, since we have nothing to unpack, let's take a walk around the ship. Is this one of your East Indiamen?"

"It is," Harry replied and took her arm for the stroll on deck. Many memories of his first and other voyages came to his mind and he regaled her with these stories until the dinner bell sounded.

After dinner Agnes left the table with the other women, while Harry stayed for the traditional round of whiskey provided by the captain. When the opportunity presented itself, he quietly inquired of the captain if everything had gone according to plan. Assured that it had, Harry excused himself and headed to his cabin. He had some things he needed to discuss with Agnes. He only hoped he had not done wrong in waiting until now. It had seemed best to keep his plans to himself until he was sure they would come off, but now he feared Agnes might be offended at not being included in the planning. Well, what was done, was done. As it happened, he met Agnes at the door to their quarters.

"We timed that well, didn't we?" Agnes said smiling.

"We did, indeed. I only hope you are not offended by my timing in another matter, one I will tell you about once we are inside our room," Harry replied.

"How mysterious you are, Harry. What could you do that could possibly offend me?"

"I've made plans for us without consulting you, my dear. At the time I felt it was the best way." He looked so contrite that Agnes quickly put her arms around him and assured him that any plans he made would suit her just fine.

"I'll hold you to that, my love," he told her and began to explain what he had done. He had no doubt that their marriage, performed in Belem by a Roman priest, was legal in every way, but he was a life-long Episcopalian and would be more comfortable being married by an Episcopal priest. "We should have been married years ago by my friend Roger Price in King's Chapel, or perhaps in his new church in Hopkinton," he told her. When he spoke to the ship's captain at the time he arranged for passage, he mentioned his new marriage and his misgivings about it. The captain informed him that he himself was of the Episcopalian faith, though not a priest, but as captain of the ship he was authorized to perform weddings on board. Harry immediately took him up on his offer to remarry himself and Agnes. Thinking back on the circumstances of their wedding, he felt Agnes had been cheated out of the social activities normally associated with the marriage rite. He was sure she would enjoy being remarried in a more festive manner. He would surprise her by planning a wedding in the presence of the passengers aboard, and after the ceremony they would treat everyone to champagne and fruited cakes. The captain was quite willing to have his steward order the necessary supplies, so long as Harry paid for them. Harry gave the captain a note to cover these expenses.

"So, Agnes, we will be married again at sea tomorrow evening. I meant for you to be pleased by these plans. Are you?"

The mischievious imp in Agnes wanted to tease him for just a little while, but he looked so worried, she fell back on the tried and true, "Yes, Harry."

Harry was relieved and took her in his arms and thanked her profusely. When at last he let her go, she admitted to him that she was overwhelmed by his generosity and the kind impulses which had caused him to plan such a charming celebration of their love. She had never expected to be a bride at all, certainly not twice.

"You were and will again be the most beautiful bride ever," Harry told her.

"As well as the most tattered and torn," she replied. Her imp had its way after all.

CHAPTER 20

▼

If Agnes had not expected her first wedding to Sir Harry nor the second one now just hours away, she was not yet done with surprises. There were many more coming her way. Despite her excitement over the coming event, she slept soundly that first night aboard the ship, as did Harry. The next morning proved to be warm and sunny, and the ocean was far calmer than it had been such a short time ago on the day of the terrible earthquake. The couple ate heartily at breakfast and enjoyed conversations with other guests at the captain's table.

When the captain stood up, the ladies took their leave, heading off to their cabins for a morning of reading or sewing. The gentlemen, of course, remained at the table to enjoy cigars and a glass or two of port from the bottles provided by the captain. Agnes was startled to hear her named called out by a woman she had not yet met. "Lady Frankland, may I have a word with you?" asked an elderly woman with steel grey hair wound tightly in a knot at the top of her head. She was wearing a dress of fine green wool and Agnes immediately recognized her air of aristocracy. The woman introduced herself as Isobel Wainwright. "Lady Frankland, I think it is just grand that you and your handsome husband are renewing your wedding vows on board our ship tonight. What a lovely idea."

Agnes, pleased to be approached by the woman, explained the circumstances of their first wedding and that Harry dearly wanted to be wed by an Episcopal clergyman.

"Lady Frankland, although you and I have not previously met, my husband and I were friends of Sir Thomas Frankland for many years. My husband, Oliver, was also a navy man, you see. We live in the West Riding of Yorkshire, but have traveled to Great Thirkleby Hall many times for dinners and dances. We knew both of Sir Thomas's wives, Elizabeth and Dinah. Both lovely women. Did you know them?"

"I'm sorry to say I did not meet Elizabeth or Sir Thomas. I expect to meet the present Lady Frankland when we get to England."

"Lady Frankland, please do not take offense at what I am about to say. I mean it in the most friendly way."

"I'm quite sure you do, Lady Wainwright. Please say what is on your mind."

"I am quite aware that you and your husband were caught in the thick of that terrible earthquake and that you lost most of your possessions."

"That's quite true, Lady Wainwright. It was horrible. We did lose our possessions, but I am forever grateful that I did not lose my dearest Harry."

"Of course you are, my dear. I would feel the same about my Oliver. He and I lived several miles out from the worst destruction of the earthquake. In fact our home was basically unscathed by it. Oliver and I were not at home at the time, being on holiday in Italy to visit friends now staying in Florence, or as they call it there, Firenze. This brings me in a roundabout way to the subject which I wished to talk about with you. You see, while in Florence, I was introduced to an excellent dressmaker. Her reputation was so fine and she had such beautiful fabrics in her workroom, that I'm afraid I bought far more frocks for my daughter Sylvia than I should have. Did I tell you that Sylvia and Sir Thomas's older daughter Betty have been good friends since their school days? In fact, each was in the other's wedding party."

"You didn't mention that. It's a fine coincidence that you and I should meet in this way, isn't it?"

"Yes, Lady Frankland, it is. And perhaps it's a coincidence or even something ordained that I was led to buy too many frocks for Sylvia. I should be very much pleased if you would accept one of them to wear at your wedding this evening."

"Oh, Lady Wainwright, I believe you have noticed the torn and tattered condition of the one I have been wearing for nearly two weeks. I should be so grateful to accept your generous offer. Of course, I'll have Harry give you a note to cover its cost."

"Nothing of the sort, Lady Frankland. It will be my wedding gift to you. When can you come to my cabin and choose the one you like best? Would now be good?"

"As they say, there's no time like the present. I expect our husbands will be smoking and sharing stories for another hour or more."

"Lady Frankland, I would like you to call me Isobel."

"Thank you, Lady Wainwright, and as much as I have enjoyed hearing myself called 'Lady Frankland', please call me Agnes."

As the two women arrived at Isobel's cabin, Isobel told Agnes that her daughter Sylvia was almost exactly the same size as Agnes herself, even though she, Isobel, was a good three inches taller and probably thirty pounds heavier. She opened a large steamer trunk and began to lay out the new frocks on her bed. They were each exquisitely lovely and beautifully made. Agnes could not decide among them. "They are so lovely, Isobel. Are you absolutely sure you want to part with one of them? Will Sylvia be cross if you do?"

"Agnes, Sylvia has more frocks than she has places to wear them. She doesn't need one more, let alone five, and she will not be cross for two reasons. One is that she is not a cross person. The other reason is that I shall not mention whichever one you choose. May I say that dark burgundy taffeta would look especially fine on you. Why don't you try it on first for fit?"

"Thank you, Isobel. I think if it fits properly, that would be perhaps the best choice of all. You have a good eye for color."

She took off her tattered outfit and stood before the mirror on Lady Wainwright's wall to admire the burgundy taffeta. She heard Lady Wainwright draw in her breath. "You look absolutely gorgeous, Agnes. I'm sure that's the one for you. However, you may try them all if you like or if you are not sure."

"I think you are right, Isobel, this is the one. I can hardly wait to see Harry's face when he sees me in this. Can we manage to keep this a secret until tonight? We have two of our servants with us on board ship, and Hannah is very good at fixing my hair. Could we come to your cabin shortly before the wedding to get me ready?"

"Of course, my dear. There's nothing I like better than a little subterfuge, especially if the joke is on someone's husband, mine or anyone else's. I'll have Oliver invite Sir Charles to the dining room early for a round of drinks with the gentlemen in honor of his pending marriage, or, in this case, remarriage."

"Thank you. I think I hear the men coming back. I'll scurry to my cabin before Harry gets there and wonders what I'm up to. I'll be over with Hannah this afternoon."

Agnes had barely closed the door to their cabin when Harry came in. "Did you have a pleasant morning with the gentlemen, Harry?" she asked.

"I did. I hope you didn't mind being left alone."

"Not at all. I spent the time thinking about our wedding this evening."

"Then perhaps now is the time for me to give you this," Harry told her as he took a long velvet box out of his frockcoat pocket. "Close your eyes and turn your back to me," he ordered.

Agnes did as she was bidden, and Harry placed a string of lustrous pearls around her neck, pushing her shining black hair out of the way while he closed the golden clasp. "Now you may look." She had no mirror in their cabin, but she could see her reflection in the window. "Oh, Harry, it's beautiful. How did you come up with it? I thought all the shops were closed in both Lisbon and Belem."

"I had Captain Everett get it for me. He is very clever about finding things that other people would not be able to get. He knows a great many merchants and is always welcome in their shops or in their homes if their shops are closed. Beyond that I cannot tell you much. I just hope you like it. I thought it would take your mind off your tattered dress."

"I shall cherish it forever, Darling. Oh, Harry, you are so good to me, and I love you so much."

"No more than I love you, Agnes, my lovely wife." A discreet knock on their door prevented any further words or other expressions of love. It was Oliver Wainwright, come to ask Harry to join him and the other gentlemen for drinks at five o'clock.

Agnes was pleased that her new friend Isobel didn't waste any time putting her plans into action. Harry turned to her and asked if she minded. She told him it would allow her to get ready without interruption and that she would meet him in the dining room at six o'clock.

Sir Wainwright left and the couple resumed their expressions of affection. After their excellent dinner at 2 p.m., they strolled about the deck. Harry touched his hat whenever an officer passed by, as he had been taught so long ago by his father in Bengal. He showed Agnes the station he had been assigned to by the Bill of Quarters. "Only in case we're attacked by pirates. Our good captain assures me this vessel has not been so maligned in twenty years at sea. I sincerely hope her record remains unbroken."

"I believe our earthquake was enough excitement to last both of us a long time," Agnes told him and added, "Although it did result in our marriage. At least some good came from that terrible event."

"I shall ever be vexed that it took an earthquake to bring me to my senses. One would think a simple knock on the head would have sufficed." He laughed as he reached for her waist and drew her to him.

"Had I but known, I could have performed that service for you," Agnes told him with a sober look on her face which immediately dissolved into laughter.

Promptly at five o'clock, Harry and Oliver Wainwright met in the dining room in the ship's cuddy. As soon as he was out of sight, Agnes and Hannah hurried to Lady Wainwright's cabin. They were surprised to find several other women present. Isobel quickly explained. "My dear, these ladies are all as excited as I about your wedding ceremony, and each has brought you a token to add to your joy on this happy occasion."

Each woman was introduced. The first gave Agnes some pink roses from a bouquet in her cabin. "My favorite flower," Agnes exclaimed. "How thoughtful of you."

Others brought her lace-edged handkerchiefs, a pair of embroidered hose, a small vial of perfume, some stationery, the remainder of a box of chocolates—whatever they could find on such short notice. Agnes was nearly overcome with gratitude. With tears glistening in her eyes she thanked one and all profusely.

"Now scoot along," Isobel told the ladies, "our bride must get herself ready. We'll see you all again at six." Agnes again expressed her thanks, and the ladies left.

Isobel was quick to notice the pearls Agnes was wearing and admired them and the ingenuity of Harry and the captain in obtaining them. "Men can be so clever on occasion," she said. "Of course, there are other occasions which we shall not discuss at this time."

Agnes shook her head and smiled at this wise and witty woman. She saw the burgundy dress lying on Isobel's bed along with a complete set of undergarments.

"Where did these come from," she asked.

"I purchased them along with the frocks for my daughter. I thought you could use them."

"You cannot imagine how pleased I am to be able to go to my wedding in all this new finery. Thank you, Isobel. You certainly have been a good friend to one you just met."

"We may have just met, but I was drawn to you as soon as I saw you. I mean this in a motherly way. You seem like another daughter to me."

"Then you shall stand for my own mother at the ceremony, Isobel. How I wish she could be here. She has yet to hear that I am at last Lady Frankland. I hope to be able to tell her soon. Harry's mother has not heard the good word yet either. I must tell you, Isobel, I was not warmly received by Harry's family and friends when we met. Poor Harry, he didn't marry me because he felt his people would be offended because I am of lower birth, but as it turned out, they were offended because we were not married."

"They sound a snobbish lot," Isobel told her. "I think they should have showered you with good will and love."

Agnes smiled as she pulled the burgundy dress up over her body. It was such a perfect fit, it might have been made expressly for her. Though she had thought it was made for her daughter, Isobel wondered again if somehow it had always been intended for Agnes Frankland.

Promptly at six, Agnes entered the dining room, followed by Lady Wainwright. The look on Harry's face was all she could have hoped for. At first he seemed stunned. When he recovered, he smiled broadly and turned to the assembled guests and asked, "Is she not a beautiful bride?" The guests applauded while Agnes blushed happily and moved to Harry's side.

The ceremony was short, but moving. Agnes was once again presented as Lady Frankland. The ship's steward and his crew brought out the champagne and fruited cakes Harry had ordered, as the couple received warm congratulations from everyone.

"Now, if only you could wave your magic wand and produce an orchestra, we could dance," Agnes chided her husband.

"What if I just ring a bell?" he asked.

"What do you mean, Harry?" she asked, puzzled.

"You'll see." He rang a small handbell, and five crew members entered the room. One had a harmonica, one a hornpipe, one a recorder, one a piccolo, and the last a small drum. The man with the harmonica stepped forward. He appeared to be the leader of this odd group.

"Ladies and Gennulmen, on this happy occasion, we will be providin' the music for yer entertainment. We ain't often had the pleasure of playing afore sech a elegant group of folks, but we do a fine hornpipe and some reels, contra dances and round dances. I'm afraid we don't know any minuets or the like."

"Thank heavens for small favors," Harry whispered to Agnes, who made an expression of mock disappointment. Nothing could really disappoint her on this wonderful night.

The group began a hornpipe dance, named for the instrument one of the sailors played. Another group of sailors came forth and danced to the music, putting the guests, however aristocratic, in a dancing mood. While it was not their usual fare, they all participated in the reels and contras, having a happy and spirited time until the bell for their evening meal sounded at 9 p.m.

Back in their cabin that night Harry and Agnes stayed awake for hours, talking about all the wonderful surprises and events of their second wedding night.

C H A P T E R   2 1

▼

The Franklands and their fellow passengers were blessed with good weather for the remainder of their trip to England. There were no pirate attacks or threats from vessels of other nations. No storms, no seasickness. Because of the party atmosphere of their remarriage on board, all the passengers in the roundhouse and lower cabins recognized the couple wherever they went. They soon became involved in an extended group of genteel travelers. Harry continued to meet with the men after breakfast for cigars and conversation. Agnes and the other women visited regularly in each others cabins, sometimes playing games, sometimes knitting or embroidering, always chatting merrily away. In the evening they were joined by the men for more cards.

Captain Everett, having seen how much his passengers enjoyed the makeshift band of sailors, brought them forth each night for more music and dancing. The ladies, led by Isobel Wainwright, agreed never to mention these "common" evenings once they reached England and returned to the diversions of high society. Nevertheless, they had a good time, and Agnes confessed to Harry when they were alone in their cabin that she had not felt so "at home" in a long time.

When at last they reached England, Harry headed immediately to the nearest tavern and arranged for lodging for the night. "If this is less than satisfactory, Agnes, we can move to another place tomorrow, but I have a great need to feel settled, if only for one night. Tomorrow we will inquire about a dressmaker for you. I am already acquainted with an excellent tailor. As astonished and pleased as I was to see you in that burgundy dress on our wedding night, I think a change would be most welcome. And, please, find a dust bin for that tattered green."

"Dear Harry, believe me, I shall be even happier than you to have some changes of clothing, although I shall keep this burgundy all my life. It is very special to me, and I shall wear it every year on our anniversary."

"I understand perfectly, my love. I plan to keep my red frockcoat with the hole in the sleeve as a reminder of three dramatic occasions in my life, the earthquake and our weddings. You see, I'm somewhat of a sentimentalist, too."

"I've known that for years, Harry," Agnes replied, embracing him lovingly.

As though Fate thought they had had enough of bad times back in Lisbon and Belem, things moved forward for the Franklands in an especially fortuitous manner in London. The following morning, after a hearty breakfast at the tavern, they traveled by carriage to Harry's tailor. He was able to recommend an excellent seamstress not more than a block away. Her name was Madam Fleet. Harry escorted Agnes to her place of business, and once he had ascertained that she was in good hands, he returned to the tailor, promising to come back for her in a few hours' time.

Agnes explained her situation to Madam Fleet, a tiny lady with frizzy once-red hair. "Ah, Lady Frankland," she said, "I think you will have only good luck from now on. In fact, I think it may start right now. You see, I have on hand several items I made for a lady who was just your size but did not have your good luck. Sadly, she passed away before she could pick up her new things. If you are not superstitious about wearing garments made for a person who died, I could let you have them now, so that you could have clothing to wear during your stay in London. Of course, if you do not like any of them, you are under no obligation to buy them. I just thought it might work out for you."

"Madam Fleet," Agnes replied, "at this point, I'd be grateful for clothes made for a witch, dead or alive. Please let me see them."

As Madam Fleet had predicted, the dresses fit Agnes perfectly. Agnes had no hesitation in buying them then and there. "As soon as my husband comes back for me, he'll give you his note to pay for them. Thank you, so much. You can't imagine how I've longed for a fresh wardrobe."

The next hours passed quickly as Agnes chose fabrics, patterns and colors for the clothes she would have made for their stay in England. She was awed by the number and variety of the bolts of fabric piled high on two long tables along the side of the room. She saw silks of changeable colors, floral patterns and stripes. There was red baize for underpetticoats, thin silk and hair Bengal, twilled bombazine made of silk and worsted, Alapeen in two varieties, some a combination of silk and wool, the others combining mohair and cotton. Agnes knew immediately on seeing it that one dress would be made of challis, probably the rich blue shade. She would also have a special gown for parties in rose-colored watered grogram and another dress in French green paragon. To complete her wardrobe she ordered a nightgown of satinette and a flowing negligee of white lutestring.

Since the temperature in November in England was at least twelve or thirteen degrees colder than in Lisbon, she asked that a good wool coat be the first garment for Madam Fleet to work on. She could manage nicely with the burgundy and the deceased lady's lovely outfits for the few days Madam Fleet would need to complete the first of her new things. She would ask Harry to find a shoemaker. The shoes she was wearing the day she rescued him were wearing thin both top and bottom. Ah, it would feel so good to be nicely dressed again.

Harry had had a very successful visit with his tailor, deciding on fine leather for breeches and a jacket for fox hunts. He felt a waistcoat of tan and brown calamanco would be very useful as well as good looking. It was a wool fabric, glossy, with a satin twill. He wondered how the checkered pattern was woven so as to be seen only on one side of the material. In addition, he ordered a coat and waistcoat in grey Duroy, Kersey stockings for himself and Agnes, yellow nankeen breeches, a waistcoat of blue paduasoy, several other breeches and finally a warm wool cloak lined in scarlet Ratteen. He shared Agnes' thought that it would feel good to once again be properly dressed.

For the next week Harry contacted acquaintances and business friends in London. He was particularly pleased to make the transactions necessary to allow all the notes he had written since the earthquake to be redeemed. It also felt good to have currency in his pocket once more. He was still wearing the red coat and grey breeches he had on during the earthquake, but he had given up his freshly powdered wig that very day, as it was in as poor condition as the dress Agnes wore for so long. Besides ordering a complete wardrobe from his tailor, he visited London's most skilled shoemaker along with Agnes. He would also see a peruke-maker. They returned daily to pick up whatever items the various shops had completed.

The remainder of their time they visited places of interest in and around London. Harry enjoyed once again many of the places he had first seen with his Uncle Thomas what seemed like a lifetime ago. Each place appeared more beautiful, more interesting, more amazing this time. It must be because Agnes was with him, he thought, once more remembering how his father had enjoyed his first trip to India so much because he had been accompanied by his wife.

Harry found himself as pleased and excited to show her the sights of London as she was to see them. They delighted in walking across the nearly new Westminster Bridge across the Thames (1747) and observing the lovely view from that vantage point. They could see the nearby palace built by Edward the Confessor and Westminster Abbey where many of the English kings were crowned and buried.

Agnes was in awe of the marble whiteness of James Gibbs' fine St. Mary-le-strand Church. Built around 1715, its tiered steeple and lovely columns on two levels were like a fantasy to the daughter of a Marblehead fisherman.

They crossed the Old London Bridge by carriage. It had more the feel of a street than a bridge since houses and a chapel were added to it long after it was begun in 1176. Agnes was delighted to see the Yeoman Warders, called by some "beefeaters", at the Tower of London. Harry told her the Tower was begun by William the Conqueror nearly 700 years earlier. While she was impressed by the age of the building, she was more enchanted by the Warders' bright red Tudor tunics and black hats decorated in red, white and blue. Harry brought her one evening to watch the Ceremony of the Keys, a nightly ritual performed by the Warders.

Another lovely building to be seen from the river was Lambeth Palace, the residence of the Archbishop of Canterbury. Agnes thanked Harry gratefully. "I never knew there were so many wonderful things to see in London," she told him.

"There are many more, Agnes. We will view them another time," Harry replied.

As soon as they both had proper clothing to wear, they accepted invitations to visit several of the families Harry had known when he lived at Great Thirkleby Hall. He smiled to himself as he thought how relieved he'd been on board ship that the motley crew did not play minuets. Now, at a party in the home of Horace Walpole, 4th Earl of Oxford, and his friend of many years, he realized how proudly he did that "foppish" dance with Agnes on his arm. Ah, Agnes, he thought, you'll never know all you have done for me, not the least of which was saving my life.

At the end of the next week, they had sufficient clothes, shoes, wigs, undergarments and accessories for their visit to Harry's mother. They would pick up the rest of the things they ordered when they were next in London. They hired a carriage and two bay horses and were off to Mattersea. Agnes did her best not to show her anxiety over revisiting the family members and friends who had treated her so uncivilly at her last visit. Would the fact that she was now Lady Frankland make a difference, or would they make snide remarks to the effect that she had snared her baronet at last? Harry seemed so serene and was obviously looking forward to seeing his sisters and brothers and their mother, that she did not speak of her own fears and doubts.

Harry surprised her by asking if she was hesitant about returning. "A little," she confessed.

"I promise you, Lady Frankland, I shall not stand by again and have you neglected and mistreated. It is to my everlasting shame that I failed to intervene before. You will not be subjected to such common behavior again."

"I never blamed you, Harry. I did wonder how one as kind and gentlemanly as you sprung from such a family, but I held only them responsible for their actions. You have nothing to be ashamed of on my behalf. Not one single thing."

"Thank you. You relieve me of some of my shame, but I repeat my promise that I will not let such behavior go unchallenged again."

Harry had sent word to Mattersea that they would be arriving late in the afternoon. He was confident that his mother would have everything in readiness for them, including an excellent meal. He did not, however, expect to find so many family members on hand as were there to welcome them.

The elder Lady Frankland moved straight to the new Lady Frankland and, with tears of gratitude in her eyes, embraced her as she would her own daughter.

"My dear Agnes, I can never thank you enough for saving my son's life, and, I may add, his character. On behalf of myself and all the Franklands, I apologize to you for our most unaristocratic treatment of you when you were here before. Can you forgive us?"

Agnes noted with amusement the woman's choice of the word 'unaristocratic'. "Lady Frankland, let us speak no more of that time. We shall start anew. You are Harry's family, and I am quite willing to have a loving and congenial relationship with all of you who wish the same."

"Wherever did you find this woman, Harry? She is indeed worthy of the name Lady Frankland."

"Yes, Mother, I told Agnes just the other day that I was sure you and the others would have come to your senses by now," Harry said with one of his teasing smiles.

"I see you haven't changed a bit, my dearest son. And I'm delighted to once again be treated to your unique brand of teasing. I just wish your dear father could be here to see what a fine man you have become and what a charming and lovely lady you have married."

The happy couple spent full days sightseeing, visiting and attending parties in their honor. Harry scanned the newspapers for word of the progress in Lisbon.

He was having a wonderful time in England, but the winter was too cold for his taste, and he longed to return to the life of leisure and pleasure he and Agnes had enjoyed in Portugal.

They arrived in Lisbon in April of 1756 and rented a house from one Don Gaston, hired a housekeeper named Anne Foley, and delivered to her care, among other things, 21 table cloths, 24 napkins, and 24 towels, according to his journal, in which he had once again begun to write. Their former landlord, Mr. Coles, still grieving moistily for his daughter who died in the carriage she and Harry were riding in when the earthquake struck, had spent days picking through the rubble of the rented house. In addition to the items Harry had hidden away before leaving for Belem, Mr. Coles had found a few more of their possessions in usable condition. Since it was a fully-furnished rented home, Harry and Agnes had brought few of their own things from Boston. However, they had purchased some items in Lisbon to "make it seem like our place". Agnes was especially delighted to once more see the small table with inlaid wood designs Harry had brought home to her as a house-warming gift. Mr. Coles had also found her tortoise shell comb, her hand mirror which had a long scratch on the glass but was otherwise in good condition, and the buckles from a pair of her shoes. Harry's new-found possessions included his chess set, the silver box in which he kept playing cards, and, surprisingly, several of his books, which must have been protected by the beams that kept the worst of the rubble away from them. When he spoke to Mr. Coles of his astonishment concerning what items survived and what supposedly sturdy items were destroyed, Mr. Coles related story after story of similar situations all over Lisbon.

While it was sad to see daily the unrestored buildings and the piles of debris all around, they were delighted to return to the circle of friends they had known before. The English community had been particularly fortunate during the horror of the earthquake. Compared to the native citizens, they lost few of their number. Perhaps their near escape caused both groups of people to sieze the day and make the most of what time would be allotted to them. The Franklands soon found themselves invited to a round of parties and events that could only be described as strenuous.

Agnes especially enjoyed a few days' respite in northeast Portugal in the town of Murca, where she was enchanted by the porcos left there, Harry told her, by the Celtic people who drifted into the Iberian peninsula across the western passes of the Pyrenees Mountains in the 10th century B.C. The porcos were rudely carved stone statues of boars. They were not unique to Murca, but remnants of them have been found on nearly every mountain top in northern Portugal. It was said criminals were tied to such structures in many Portuguese towns in those days. The country people regarded them with a mixture of humor and awe.

The Celts were known to be good farmers, and they cultivated the land to grow wheat for bread, barley for beer and flax for linen clothing. For their own defense against marauders of any sort, they built their round stone houses on the highest parts of the areas where they lived, just as the early settlers in Agnes' Marblehead had built their homes and meeting houses on the highest parts of that town. It is believed the Moors introduced the peculiar squeaking cart with an axle that turns with the wheel, which the Franklands saw in use on some farms they passed by.

Agnes, who had considered the word "old" to mean from the 17th century when it was applied to buildings and other man-made structures in America, was awed by the sights she saw in Portugal. Their trip to Sintra was both frightening and restful. The hairpin bends on the steep, narrow roads wound through dense forests, areas of moss-covered boulders, and magnificent views of the Atlantic before coming to country roads and small villages on the cool green northern slopes of Serra de Sintra. The Palace at Sintra was left from the early Moorish occupation. Waterwheels they saw in the valley of the Mondego below Coimbra were thought to be left over from the irrigated estates of the settlers from Persia as early as 700-800. Even the name of Portugal had its roots in the Moorish occupation. The term "Provincia Portucalence" was used to define the lands reconquered from the Moors between the Douro and Minho Rivers. It was King Afonso Henriques, crowned in 1143 at the church of Santa Maria de Almacave in Lamego, who called the area Portugal in 1139, and it was he who recaptured Lisbon in 1147.

Although the Black Death (the Plague) reduced the population of Portugal to less than a million in 1348, King Fernando rebuilt Lisbon during his 1362-1383 reign, and soon there were as many as 450 ships moored in the Tagus with more arriving daily as traders came to buy and sell and others sought work in the renewed city. By the 16th century, Portugal had become the richest and most beautiful nation on earth and Lisbon the richest capital. In 60 B.C. Lisbon, then called Olisipo, was the western capital of the Roman Empire. As they had done all over their empire, the Romans left a network of roads across the area which eventually became the basis of expressways linking Portugal to Spain and the rest of Europe.

When Harry had business in the south, in the Algarve area, Agnes was once again fascinated by the Moorish fortifications, filigreed chimneys, and the azulejos (tiles) on the exteriors of churches and manor houses. In season it was a delight to have fresh oranges, figs and almonds which were grown in the area.

These excursions, delightful as they were would not continue. It appears that staying settled in any one place was not in the grand plan for the Franklands' lives. Their stay in Lisbon was nearing its end. The call of business from Boston caused them to sail in just a few months from Belem on the ship Friendship with Captain Eleazor Johnson in command.

CHAPTER 22

▼

On their arrival in Boston, Agnes found the attitude of society towards her had changed completely. When she left, she was condemned by citizens ranging from the aristocracy to school children on the street for her living arrangement in Harry Frankland's home. Now, as Lady Frankland, her presence was sought after by one and all. She soon became one of the leading hostesses of the day, and Harry began his search for a more suitable house to entertain in. What he was looking for soon came available, the splendid Clarke mansion on Garden Court and Bell Alley in the prestigious north end of Boston.

The house had been built by William Clarke, one of the wealthiest of Boston's merchants. It was sold in 1746 to Thomas Greenough for 1400 pounds. Harry got it for 1200 pounds sterling in 1756 and was well pleased with his bargain. The elegant and commodious house was made of brick and stood three stories tall. There were twenty-six beautifully designed rooms in all with a center staircase in the downstairs hallway so wide and so easily mounted that Harry, in one of his more playful moods, actually rode his pony up the stairs.

Lady Frankland busied herself finding just the right furniture for the parlors which boasted elaborately carved and fluted columns and sumptuously gilded pilasters and cornices. Beautiful landscape scenery could be enjoyed above the wainscotted walls. The porcelain fireplaces sported mantels of Italian marble. The eastern parlor was especially admired for its floor of inlaid diamond-shaped figures with a marvelous center design made of some three hundred different kinds of wood around the coat of arms of the original owners, the Clarke family.

As beautiful as this house was, the Franklands did not spend all of their time there. They continued to frequent their home in Hopkinton, and on one trip back to Boston from a weekend in the country, they had another hair-raising experience, although not of the caliber of the earthquake they endured in Portugal. As the "New Hampshire Gazette" of September 2, 1757, recounts the story: "Thursday last as Sir Henry Frankland and his lady were coming into town in their chariot, a number of boys were gunning on Boston neck (notwithstanding there is an express law to the contrary) when one of them discharging his piece at a bird, missed the same, and almost the whole charge of shot came into the chariot where Sir Henry and his lady were, several of which entered his hat and clothes, and one grazed his face, but did no other damage to him or (his) lady."

As busy as their lives were in Boston and Hopkinton, they were not yet done with world travel. Harry's health was beginning to decline in the summer of 1757, and he told Agnes, "My dear, I think we need to go to a warmer climate."

"Do you mean to go south from here?" she asked.

"I wonder what you think of an idea I've had," he replied. "If you would consider returning to Portugal despite the experience we had there on our last visit, I thought I would ask King George to make me his Ambassador to that country."

Agnes hesitated only a moment before assuring him she would go wherever he wanted to go. "You would be an excellent ambassador, Harry. You speak Portuguese fluently, and you are well aware of laws and regulations in that country, but what about your position as collector of the Port of Boston?"

"I would have to resign that, I'm sure. But that's all right. I have reaped many benefits from that position over the years; now it is time for someone else to take it over."

In July 1757, notice of Harry's appointment as consul general at Lisbon was reported in the "London Magazine". Harry's journal lists some of the items he would pack for their move to Lisbon. They included one large case filled with one small box of china figures, India dressing case, silver tea chest, backgammon table with silver ewer and shaving bason (sic), microscope, dessert ornaments, Chelsea china, one pair white netts for horses; parasol silk, Italian prints, paper, silver shaving bason, book of maps, silver knives and forks, boxes and wafers. As always, his interests and belongings were an eclectic lot. Once in London he planned to purchase "silver castors, wine glasses like Pownal's, two turreens, saucers for water glasses, dessert knives and forks and spoons, common tea kettle, jelly and syllabub glasses, fire grate, long dishes, tea cups, etc., clothes, etc., for Lady Frankland, Consul's seal, combs, mahogany tray, press for table linen and sheets, stove for flat irons, glass for live flea for microscope, Hoyle's Treatise on Whist, Dr. Dodridge's Exposition on the New Testament, 16 handsome chairs, with 2 settees, and 2 card tables, and a working table like Mrs. F. F. Gardner's." It could never be said that Harry Frankland did not know what he wanted. He liked to be prepared for every eventuality. He even had with him a recipe for costiveness, a nicer word for constipation. This consisted of "one spoonful of sulphur and oyl of sweet almonts, mixt, to be taken over night". He recorded his directions for folding a great coat: "lay it in small circumference; just spread it on the ground and double it square; then double from feet part to shoulder part, then the sides turn up about 3 feet each; then two persons roll up and tie it". His simple way to make leather boots soft and supple, was to rub them a little distance from the fire with neats foot oyl with his hand.

Harry and Agnes boarded the Mermaid at 6 p.m. on February 7 for the voyage to England. This vessel had had its share of illustrious passengers, having been under the command of Captain Douglas when she took the Vigilant on May 18, 1745. The ship was also the one on which Rev. Roger Price sailed to England in 1747. Unfortunately, it would be lost near the Bahama Islands on June 24, 1760. However, Harry and Agnes made it safely to London, and they were in Lisbon once more by June, where they were honored guests at the wedding of the Infanta Don Pedro when he married the princess Dona Maria from Brazil. Following that festive occasion, the Franklands spent the remainder of the summer at Caldas de Rainha to enjoy the waters which were impregnated with sulphureted hydrogen and maintained a very pleasant temperature of 92 degrees F. In fact, they would spend several summers there, where Harry enjoyed riding, hunting, botanizing, reading and playing his old favorite game of whist with Lady Frankland and their most congenial friends.

As for all of Harry's travel plans, the visits to Caldas required their own specific provisions. His journal lists: guns, powder, shot, rammer to wash guns, flints, shot pouches, powder horn, fine emery, neats foot oyl, turn screw, dog chains, and padlock, large powder flask, saddle and bridle for little macho, ditto for Lady Frankland, (we assume here he referred to her horse), almanack, pens, ink, paper, memorandum book, almont powder, hammers, chisels, nails, and corks. The trip from Lisbon to Caldas lasted from 5:30 a.m. to 8:10 p.m. It was well worth the ride for Harry to spend time in the bath there, although privacy was not one of the benefits offered. The bath was 46 palms long, 13 palms broad and could contain 60 persons at a time.

In 1761 Harry critiqued the new comedy "All in the Wrong," by Mr. Arthur Murphy in his journal. "The general intention of this comedy is to point what infinite perplexities may arise in the conversation between the sexes both before and after marriage, from our readily giving way to unnecessary suspicions, even on strong appearances, without endeavoring by a cool and discreet conduct to come to such as may be necessary for the clearing up of our doubts and restoring that peace of mind which a contrary conduct must unavoidably destroy." There was no indication that he and Agnes suffered such perplexities.

Surprisingly, Harry had an opinion on fashion, writing "when a fashion has become almost universal, though it may appear ridiculous to you, it is best to comply, and not to appear too singular in your own opinion." Singular or not, Harry had an opinion on just about everything. He wrote: "The best books to learn (sic) children to read English are, "A New Guide to the English Tongue," by Thomas Disworth; "The Royal English Grammar", by James Greenwood, and "The Spelling Dictionary of the English Language" with a compendious English Grammar prefixed." Unfortunately, Harry's own best student, Agnes, could read well but never did master spelling.

All their activities and sudden changes in the weather resulted in Agnes catching a bad cold with a sore throat. They called in Dr. Wade who prescribed a gargle made of "marsh mallows and figs boyled together with a little warm milk added."

The Franklands' travelling days were coming to an end at last. Following a short visit in Boston and Hopkinton, Harry realized he needed to return to Bath, England, for the healing mineral waters there. Two entries in his journal show his thoughts at that time. In Sept. he wrote, "I cannot suffer a man of low condition to exceed me in good manners." and "I endeavor to keep myself calm and sedate: I live modestly and avoid ostentation, decently, and not above my condition, and do not entertain a number of parasites who forget favors the moment they depart from my table."

Although Frankland had left Lisbon in 1763, he kept the office of consul general for several more years, being replaced in 1767 by Sir John Hort.

Harry, with his loving Agnes by his side, was bedridden for fourteen weeks as of December 9, 1767, and died on January 11, 1768 at the age of 51 years, 8 months and 1 day. Heartbroken, Agnes, Lady Frankland, watched as her friend, her lover, her husband was laid to rest in the church in Weston, near Bath. She had a loving monumental inscription placed high against the wall in the nave of the church which read: "To the memory of Sir Charles Henry Frankland of Thirkleby in the county of York, Baronet, consul general for many years at Lisbon from whence he came in hopes of recovery from a bad state of health to Bath, where after a tedious and painful illness which he sustained with patience and resignation becoming a Christian, he died 11th January 1768 in the 52 year of his life without issue and at his own desire, lies buried in this church. This monument is erected by his affectionate widow Agnes, Lady Frankland."

So ends the story of the British aristocrat and the scrub-maid from Marblehead, who, despite all odds and through all manner of events, shared a lifetime of affection and fidelity, though it took an earthquake to get them married.

Bibliography
of
IT TOOK AN EARTHQUAKE

By Miriam J. Walker

Every Day Life in The Massachusetts Bay Colony, George Francis Dow, Dover Publications 1988

The East Indiamen, by Russell Miller and the editors of Time-Life Books, Alexandria VA 1980

Sir Charles Henry Frankland by Elias Nason, J. Munsell, Publisher, 1865

The Portuguese, The Land And Its People, by Marion Kaplan, Viking, 1991

Admiral of the White, Oxford Companion to The Ships and Sea

A guide to Marblehead, by Samuel Roads, Jr., Published by Merrill H. Graves, Marblehead, Mass. 1887

Great Thirkleby, Geographical And Historical information from the year 1890, Bulmer

The Colonial Wars, by Howard H. Beckham, 1689-1762, published by University of Chicago Press 1964

The East India Company and the British Empire in the Far East, Marguerite Eyer Wilbur, Russell and Russell 1970

The Rise of the English Shipping Industry in the 17th and 18th Centuries, by Newton Abbott. David and Charles, 1962

978-0-595-40122-2
0-595-40122-8

Printed in the United States
52980LVS00005B/137

9 780595 401222